Her Only Hero

by

Judy Malcolm

Cover Art by *Kristian Norris*

The Wild Rose Press, Inc.
PO Box 708
Adams Basin, NY 14410-0708
Visit us at www.thewildrosepress.com

Publishing History
First Edition, 2024
Trade Paperback ISBN 978-1-5092-5626-6
Digital ISBN 978-1-5092-5627-3

Published in the United States of America

Dedication

For all heroes

Acknowledgements

Many thanks to my editor, Ally Robertson, and The Wild Rose Press.

Thank you to retired police captain, John Canaris, for patiently and graciously answering my many policing questions.

To Jenn MacPherson, Carlene Hambly, Corinne Fletcher, Brian Donohue, and Marla Silverthorn, thank you for sharing autopsy expertise.

I'm ever grateful to my writers' group—Magda Gold, Diane Kowalyshyn, and Tim Simmons.

Thank you to my wonderful family for your unwavering and endless support. Love you always and forever.

Chapter One

Police and Forensic Complex, Cedar Key, Ohio

When I offered to work overtime, my lab colleagues were more than willing to leave early on a Friday afternoon, and with no plans, and no life, I was more than willing to stay. I stood by the humming centrifuge, waiting for DNA samples to spin down. I slipped off a shoe and wriggled my toes. My mind wandered back to two years ago today, this last day of August.

I reached into my lab coat pocket and removed a folded, time-worn note and reread it for the umpteenth time. Emotions squeezed inside my chest, but no tears came. Beautiful promises had been reduced to just words. I ripped the sheet into two, four, eight pieces and let the bits flutter into the trash can like radioactive fallout.

The cavernous lab had become my safe place, work my focus. Unlike relationships, the lab was organized, controlled, and predictable. Though as of late, I wondered what it would be like to venture out to crime scenes and collect evidence myself. The centrifuge shut off with a click. One at a time, I removed test tubes and put them in a rack.

The main door swung open.

Officer Patrick Verbeek.

In his black uniform, he walked with smooth,

deliberate strides and impeccable posture. Secretly, I found his presence, and the way he moved, highly attractive, though he had many other positive qualities as well. He held up a green plastic bottle of my favorite aloe beverage.

His ever-assessing gaze held me—an expression that had intimidated me when we first made our acquaintances well over two years ago. But now I knew a witty personality lurked beneath a stern exterior. Still, a "smart" crook wouldn't dare lie to him.

I hobbled toward him as I slid my shoe back on and took a couple of bills from a drawer.

"Hey, Officer. You're working late too?" I handed him the money for the bottle. "Thank you for this. I needed a boost."

He glanced at his palm and then back at me. "Why won't you allow me to buy you a drink?" he said softly. "It's just aloe juice, not a cocktail."

He was right. I hadn't let him treat me to anything— not a donut, not a coffee, and certainly not a date— though he had tried, often. His dark brows furrowed over his sapphire eyes.

"Here," he said and leaned close to me. Only my diaphragm moved as I inhaled a fresh scent of lime. He touched my hip as he slipped the money into my lab-coat pocket. I took a step back.

"Please, let me do this," he said.

I stood transfixed, still feeling the tingle of his touch.

"See? That wasn't so bad, was it?"

I hesitated before shaking my head. I didn't add that the tough part was resisting his manliness. Was that a word? My pulse quickened, and my body became a radiator. Damned primitive biological response.

He looked around and leaned against the counter. "Did everyone bail on you again?" The corner of his mouth turned up—mischievous and mocking.

"I wouldn't say that." My voice sounded hoarse, and I cleared my throat. "Overtime is optional. I chose to stay."

He crossed his arms over his chest, and the cuffs of his short-sleeved shirt tightened around his biceps. My insides continued warming. I'd been single and alone for some time, and every subtle nuance of Patrick's physique affected me, despite my efforts not to react.

"Don't you have a radio? It's too quiet in here."

"Yes, there is a radio, and no, it's not too quiet. I prefer the silence." I put my drink on the counter. "So, Officer, are you working on any new exciting cases?"

"Just traffic detail today, if you want to call that exciting."

"Haha. Definitely not."

He pushed away from the bench top. "If you're almost finished, I can give you a lift home."

"Thanks, but no. I have a bus pass."

"Your car finally gave up the ghost?"

I half-smiled and put some paperwork aside. For safety reasons, Patrick had tried to talk me into getting a four-by-four. "My hatchback is great. I'm just giving the old girl a rest."

"So, seriously, how about a ride?"

Solemnly, I pressed my lips together.

He lowered his head and sighed. "All right, June Harber. I get the hint. I'm usually not this thick, but I finally get the message."

"I'm sorry." I wanted to explain, but there was no point. It would sound lame and trite if I told him I'd been

3

hurt too deeply to trust again. I had to stand by my decision to not let a man touch me again, physically or emotionally.

"I guess I'll see you around." He gave me a last glance before leaving. I returned to the rack of samples and heard the door close. This was for the best. I knew I was messed up letting a guy like that walk out without giving him a chance. But I had to keep the pieces of my heart together. The glue hadn't set yet, and I didn't know if it ever would.

I put the specimens in the fridge for the next workday, hung my lab coat on a wall hook, and washed my hands. I unclipped my ID badge from my collar and slipped it into the back pocket of my scrubs. With my purse and drink in hand, I headed out, ensuring the steel door locked behind me. The occasional squeak of my rubber-soled shoes was the only sound as I walked down the deserted hallway to the exit.

Without a sweater, the drop in temperature gave me a shiver. Fall seemed to be coming in with a vengeance. I stepped onto the sidewalk as my bus sped by. I waved and ran after it but only succeeded in being doused with gritty exhaust.

"You're early," I muttered in frustration. In the evenings, buses only ran once every hour. I dug into my purse for my cell phone to call a taxi, but the darn thing wouldn't power on.

What next?

I turned to go back to the bus stop, and in the parking lot I noticed Patrick leaning against a squad car, looking in my direction. He didn't wave or gesture for me to come over—I had made my resistive stance perfectly clear. He stood immobile with his arms crossed over his chest.

An empty stomach hindered my better judgement. I walked toward him, and his expression lightened. He opened the passenger door. He didn't gloat or smirk, he just said, "Hi."

"Hi," I said and got in. I'd never sat in a police car before and had to admit it was kind of cool. The dashboard glowed like an amusement park at night.

"Are you hungry?" he asked.

"Not really," I said, even though my stomach threatened to rumble.

"All right then." He turned on the ignition, shifted into gear, and drove out of the lot.

"You didn't ask me where I live," I said.

He glanced at me as he changed lanes. "No, I didn't. Where do you live? The west end?" he asked, pretending he didn't already know.

I giggled. "Good guess, Officer." I clutched the handles of my purse. I enjoyed Patrick's company and casual banter, so why was I nervous?

A woman's voice from dispatch squawked on the loudspeaker. "Attention sectors 45-43, 45-42. Possible disturbance at 109 Landry Road. May be an animal."

Patrick glimpsed at his watch. "I'm off duty in a few minutes, but Landry Road is only a couple of blocks away. Would you mind if we swung by?"

"Sure." I think I managed to keep a calm, casual demeanor, but my insides felt like they were dislodged by a roller coaster.

Patrick responded via speakerphone. "Affirmative, 45-43 en route." He turned on the flashing red and blue lights, and the engine roared with acceleration.

My heart thumped harder, and I tightened my seat

belt. It surprised me how he hadn't pulled over to drop me off at a roadside. "Are you sure I'm allowed to tag along?"

"You are a civilian member of the police force. It shouldn't be an issue." He made a right and then a quick left and stopped in front of a one-story home. Along the right side of the property, a hedge lined an alleyway. Patrick parked and stared at the house.

"Stay in the car, June." I recognized the same authoritative cop tone from the infamous night we first met. Before I had worked at the forensic unit, he had responded to a call at my house. At the time, he hadn't been very nice. All the more reason it amazed me how we were here together today.

"Yes, Officer sir," I said and noticed the corner of his mouth turn up before he shut the door. He scaled the wooden porch steps and knocked. No one answered. He looked in the front window and then walked to the side of the house, disappearing from view.

I tapped my fingertips on my thigh as I watched the house. No lights were on. About twenty feet away, a square blue dumpster sat near the alley entrance. Empty plastic bottles and other trash littered the ground. And then I noticed something distinctively out of place. Something brown and white, or was it red and white? The sun was setting. Was I seeing what I thought I was seeing?

Patrick still hadn't emerged from around the house. I opened the car door, stepped out, and looked around. Everything seemed okay. An occasional car drove by, and a dog barked in the distance. Whatever disturbance had happened was probably over. Not sensing any imminent danger, I approached the dumpster. The object in question became clear, and I stared at it in disbelief. It looked like a wad of paper towels soaked with blood. I'd analyzed specimens such as this, but I'd never found or collected them, until perhaps now. Of course, my speculation could have no significance at all, and this could end up being acrylic paint from a sloppy painter.

A racoon darted out in front of me. I jumped and let out a scream as it scampered into the hedge. When assured it was gone, I bent down to pick up a corner of the towel.

Like a battering ram, something, or someone, propelled me forward. My knees landed hard on the concrete, and my head thudded against the metal dumpster. Spears of pain shot through my skull, and my knees and palms burned. Dazed, I caught a glimpse of a guy running down the alley before disappearing into overgrown shrubbery.

"June!" Patrick bolted from the side of the house. "Fuck! Are you all right?"

"I'm okay." I tried to steady my voice, but it quivered. "He ran that way, into the brush. Go!"

Patrick raced down the alley with sprinter's strides before hurdling the hedge and disappearing from sight.

I touched a tender spot on my forehead. Blood beaded on my scraped palms, and both knees of my pants were ripped. I stood on shaky legs, adjusted my clothes, and looked around. The potential evidence I found was gone. The guy who shoved me had to have snatched it.

Patrick emerged from the alleyway and jogged over. "He's gone. Did you get a look at him?"

"Yes," I said.

"How tall would you say he was?"

I pictured him running away, but on my knees, it

was hard to judge. "Medium height, I think."

"And his build?"

"Thin, no wait. He seemed muscular, maybe." I cringed at how little I remembered. I tried to line up my thoughts. "He wore a long-sleeved black hoodie, though the hood slipped off when he turned to look back."

"You saw his face?"

"Yes, but he was too far. He had a buzz cut though, blond hair, or maybe it was brown. Oh my God, why can't I remember?"

"It's ok. Come on." He cupped my elbow and guided me to the cruiser. I angled away from his touch.

"That guy," I said, trying to focus. "I think he stole evidence."

"What evidence?"

"On the ground, I saw what looked to be a blood-soaked paper towel. He must have knocked me over to grab it."

He cursed under his breath. "I shouldn't have answered this call. Please, get in the car."

"What's going on?" I said and slid in.

"There's a dead man inside."

My body trembled.

Patrick bent down to look at me. "I'm calling this in, and as soon as back-up arrives, I'm taking you to St. Eugene's Hospital."

"No," I said. Troubled memories of when I had worked at that hospital flooded in.

He got in the cruiser. "You could be concussed, June. It's better to be safe than sorry."

"Please, don't make me go back there." I squeezed my eyes shut and held my breath to stave off the irrational racing of my heart and mind.

Chapter Two

"June? Can you hear me?" Patrick's voice guided me out of my panicked thoughts. "That's it. Take deep breaths. Good job."

Strapped in the car's bucket seat, I had nowhere to hide from my embarrassment, or from Patrick's intense look of concern. His knitted brows framed his penetrating blue eyes. A warmth swirled in my stomach, and I fought through my speechlessness. "Sorry about freaking out there." I cringed. "Good thing you're trained on how to deal with people in all forms of crises."

"Don't apologize. After what happened, you're coping exceptionally well. Are you in pain? How is your head?"

"Still throbbing a bit."

"Would you be willing to go to a walk-in clinic instead of the hospital? You really should get assessed." He leaned in closer and checked my pupils. I froze. When he receded, I let out my breath. Patrick clicked a ball-point pen and wrote in a notebook until another squad car pulled in front of ours. "I'll be right back." He met with two officers, and as he spoke, he pointed to the dumpster and then toward the alleyway. They walked to the house and disappeared to the rear of the property.

I slumped in the seat, closed my eyes, and longed to be home, soaking in a hot bath with Epsom salts. Or maybe I would indulge and use a capful of my special eucalyptus bubble bath. I remembered the promising spring day it was given to me with a note saying he was always thinking of me. An ache stabbed inside, and I snapped my eyes open.

Patrick strode toward the car and got in. "You and I are finished here, June. Have you decided where you'd like me to take you? St. Eugene's? Or a walk-in? Or I could drive you home, though I advise against it."

"Let's go to St. Eugene's," I said, agreeing only because of the off chance of needing a CT scan. But for me, that hospital had too many memories and secrets trapped in its walls—both amazing and horrible.

We arrived too soon and pulled up to the emergency entrance.

"Ready?"

"As I'll ever be," I said unconvincingly.

We walked into the building. His presence by my side was comforting. He remained close as the triage nurse measured my blood pressure, temperature, and oxygen saturation, after which we moved to a curtained area. In a short amount of time, a woman entered, wearing OR greens and a stethoscope around her neck.

"Hello, I'm Dr. Carter." She had straight, light brown hair hooked behind her ears. Her eyebrows furrowed and then released. "Can you tell me what happened, June? I understand you had a spill."

"Yes. Someone shoved me to the ground and banged my head in a dumpster bin."

Dr. Carter squinted. "Oh, dear. Let's have a look." She moved my hair aside and examined my forehead. "You have a bit of a hematoma." She shone a light into my eyes. "Are you dizzy or nauseated?"

"No."

"Did you lose consciousness?"

I shook my head. "No."

"She may have been a bit confused," Patrick said.

I cringed. But he was right.

"I think further investigation is warranted," Dr. Carter said. "There's a blood test that detects TBI—traumatic brain injury. I'll get that ordered. And I'll have the nurse disinfect your wounds and apply dressings." She examined the caked blood on my forearm.

"It's strange," I said. "I don't feel this cut at all."

"Hmm, this is odd," Dr. Carter said.

"Odd? How do you mean?" I asked.

Patrick moved closer.

"I see no abrasions or contusions on your skin," the doctor said. She tilted her head. "June, I don't think this blood is yours."

"Not my blood?" My stomach turned.

"I'll clean it to check for sure," the doctor said.

"Excuse me, Doctor," Patrick said. "I'd like to submit what is cleaned off for evidence. Could I trouble you for sterile water, gauze, and a container?"

Dr. Carter nodded. "Of course. I'll be right back." She slipped out through the slit in the curtain. All of a sudden, it became silent. I glanced at Patrick. He had creases around his eyes.

"How are you holding up?" He stood like a pillar, and somehow, I drew from his strength.

"Holding fine I guess, considering I have some stranger's blood on me." I recoiled from my own arm. "I hope this blood contains nothing infectious. Who the hell was that guy?"

"That's what we're going to find out," Patrick said.

"We'll take a sample to the lab for DNA analysis. I know a lab worker who can get it done in no time." He winked.

I couldn't help but smile. His faith in my skills as a scientist lifted my mood.

Dr. Carter returned with the requested items. She reached for a box of gloves on the shelf, but Patrick stopped her.

"That's all right, Dr. Carter, I got this." He assessed the boxes of gloves. "No extra-large?"

Completely inappropriately, my mind rolled into the gutter.

The doctor rummaged through the cupboards below. "No, doesn't look like it. Sorry about that, just large. I'll leave you to it. A nurse should be in shortly."

"Thanks, Doctor," he said and grabbed a pair of the large gloves—the vinyl stretched tightly over his fingers. I tried to avert my thoughts. He poured water onto a square piece of gauze. I tensed, anticipating the coolness. When it didn't happen, I looked up at him.

"You know, this will not hurt," he said.

"I hope not." I tried to speak lightly.

When he touched the cool, wet fabric to my skin, shivers skittered up my arm. With smooth, even strokes, he wiped off all the caked blood. As suspected, the blood wasn't mine. I had no cut. He unscrewed the lid and placed the bloody gauze into the sterile jar.

"There, done," he said. "Hopefully this person's DNA is on record." He dropped the specimen container onto the mobile tray. His jaw tensed as he disinfected my arm with an alcohol wipe.

"June, I can't tell you how sorry I am for putting you in harm's way. I shouldn't have taken you on that call."

"What happened is my fault, not yours. I didn't stay

in the car like you asked."

"I should have cuffed and locked you in the back seat."

I laughed. "Maybe next time."

His lips curled up. Did he smile because I had suggested there may be a next time?

The curtain flung open, and a junior nurse entered.

"Hi, I'm Sophie. I need to take some blood and clean your wounds. Is that okay?"

"Sure," I said.

She smiled and flashed a set of straight white teeth at Patrick. He didn't seem to notice, and I almost smiled. She worked efficiently, and I cringed at being treated for minor scratches. I barely felt the needle prick when she performed the venipuncture. Later, Dr. Carter said my result was negative for a TBI, and that I should come back if I had any new or worsening symptoms.

With my forearm disinfected and my palms and knees bandaged, Patrick and I headed out. We walked down the hallway toward the exit when the elevator door opened and out stepped Victoria Silverstone—a previous co-worker. I gasped audibly. She held a large manilla envelope and looked at me with frosty green eyes. Her flawless complexion could be described as porcelain perfect, and her thin pink lips were pressed taut. I remembered how she had mastered keeping an emotionless poker face, no matter what the topic.

"Hello, June," she said in an even, pleasantly fake tone.

"Hello, Victoria," I said and kept moving. I had nothing to say to her.

I stormed through the automatic sliding doors into the chilly air. Goose bumps spread along my arms, but I welcomed them. Anything to be free of that place. Patrick caught up to me and crooked a brow without asking questions. He put the swabbed blood specimen in the trunk and opened the passenger car door.

"All set?"

I nodded.

"Time to get you home in one piece, like I originally intended."

After this evening's unimaginable events, I trusted he'd finally get me home safely.

But then again, this crazy evening wasn't over yet.

Chapter Three

Patrick parked in front of my place—a century-old home converted into two apartments. I lived on the main floor of the duplex which was adorned with antique glass bay windows in the front and at the side. I gripped the beverage bottle in my hand and looped my purse handle over my forearm.

"Thank you for the ride home," I said. "And for the adventure."

Patrick frowned. "It's very gracious of you to downplay what happened."

"I think I'm still processing it." I opened the car door. "Well, good night."

"June, could I possibly come in for a drink?"

"A drink? But you're in uniform."

"If you prefer me out of uniform, that can be arranged."

"Ha. That won't be necessary," I said. "And I'm sorry, I don't have any alcohol."

"I don't need any. A glass of water will do." He looked at the bottle in my hand. "I've always been curious about the taste of aloe."

I stretched out my arm and handed him the bottle. "Oh sure, help yourself. See you next week, at the daily grind." I exited the car and scurried up the concrete porch steps. I pushed through the exterior door and entered the foyer. My apartment door was straight ahead, and the upstairs tenant's door was on the right. I searched the depths of my handbag for my elusive keys.

"June, why are you rushing away? Are you angry?" Patrick hopped up the steps and held open the exterior door but didn't cross the entrance threshold. "I know it's late, but I want to make sure you're all right and possibly get a description of the perp while it's still fresh in your mind."

I put the key in the lock and sighed. He wasn't being unreasonable, but I was. I could be so erratic at times. "Yes, of course," I mumbled. "Please, come in."

Upon entering, hot, stifling air blanketed us. "Shoot. Sorry about the heat," I said. "The thermostat must be out of whack again." I turned on the living room lamps at both ends of the sofa. "I'll open a window."

The window latch held stiff, and Patrick lunged forward to help. Unfortunately, the sheer curtains remained motionless from the lack of a cross draft.

Seemingly unaffected by the temperature, Patrick caught sight of my wall unit with rows of music CDs, potted plants, and framed pictures.

"Are these your parents?" he asked.

"Yes."

"That's a great photo," he said. "Are they still away?"

"Yes, still on their cruise."

He kept nosing around my stuff, but oddly I didn't mind.

"I like your diverse music collection."

"Thanks."

"Would you like me to put something on?"

"No, I'd rather you didn't," I said without

explanation.

"You have a nice place, June. Neat and tasteful—like you."

It surprised me how much I valued his compliment, yet my underwhelming response was a simple, "thank you."

I went into the kitchen, and Patrick followed. I'd never had a man, other than my dad, in my kitchen, or my apartment, for that matter. Patrick's presence unnerved me, and it took a second to remember where my nice drinking glasses were. I took two down from the cabinet beside the sink, and one of them slipped out of my bandaged hand.

"Whoops," barely left my mouth when Patrick grabbed it midair. His arm brushed against mine, and something fluttered in my belly. His touch had been subtle, incidental, and completely unintentional, but my body had reacted.

"Do your hands hurt?" he said.

I glanced at the wrappings on my palms, but the bandages were only partially responsible for the glass slipping out of my hand. The other part was jitters from Patrick's proximity. "My hands feel better. But these dressings are annoying." In a swift motion, I pulled one bandage off and then the other. The scrapes were barely visible. He took my hands in his and had a look. His closeness turned my hot apartment into an oven. When he released my hands, I clasped them together and recoiled. I shouldn't have invited him in. I didn't trust my reactions to him.

"I'm relieved you escaped with minor injuries," he said. "It could have been much worse."

"But it wasn't, thankfully." I opened the freezer to

get ice and poured the drinks. I handed him a glass and guzzled from mine until it was empty. With the back of my hand, I wiped my mouth.

"Aren't you going to try it?" I asked abruptly.

He answered by putting the rim to his mouth. As he drank, I watched his Adam's apple. Powerful neck. Athletic build. Earlier he had chased the criminal with such power and speed. He was not the average male. Warmth rose to my face, and I started to perspire.

"This drink is excellent. Tastes like white grapes." He swirled the ice cubes, apparently oblivious to my "distress." "The pulp pieces are most interesting." He drank the rest and then licked his lips. His tongue seemed to move in slow motion. "Would you like to sit with me, and tell me what you remember from today? June?"

I was staring. What was wrong with me? The day's events must have had adverse effects. "Um, is it okay if we do this tomorrow?"

"Of course. I won't pressure you about the case any further. And thank you for the drink." He put the glass on the counter and caught me gazing at him again. What must he be thinking? My words and actions weren't jiving. His eyes held me spellbound. I wanted to bolt, but my legs wouldn't budge. He stepped closer and touched his lips to mine. He kissed me gently, perfectly. His lips enveloped mine. His kiss enveloped my senses.

His arms lured me into his embrace. An all-encompassing magnetic pull wanted to fuse us. I clung to reason and brought my hands to his chest and broke the bond.

Patrick looked at me with dilated pupils. He, too, appeared breathless. His usual calm expression had been replaced with one of pain? Did I look that way too?

"Too fast?" he asked in a husky voice.

Torn between body and mind, I didn't know how to respond. As cliché as it sounded, I couldn't survive the heartbreak of another failed relationship. The last one had hurt too much and even changed me. I had to protect myself because in reality, most relationships ended in destruction. But standing here, I ached for him.

When I didn't respond, Patrick lowered his head and backed away. He was halfway out of the apartment when I called out.

"Don't go."

He froze.

The next move was mine. I walked over to him, arched up, and pressed my lips to his, reigniting the wick. He placed a hand behind my neck and gently cradled my head as the kiss deepened. But then I stepped back, again. His jaw clenched, and it looked like he struggled for composure.

"Shit, June. What are you trying to do?"

He had no clue of the tug-of-war raging inside of me. I wanted to be with him, but complete intimacy could lead to overwhelming hurt. I remembered a caption I had read, and believed there was truth to it.

A loveless touch could scar your soul.

Maybe there was a way to keep things somewhat detached. I'd have to try something I'd never done before and remove the personal element of his touch. Without the element of touch, there couldn't be a complete chemical reaction.

I lowered my eyes and glanced at Patrick's utility belt. Various nylon pouches and holsters held pepper spray, a flashlight, and a gun. Then I zeroed in on the handcuffs. I unsnapped them from his belt, turning them in my hand. He crooked an eyebrow. With shaky hands, I maneuvered one end of the cuffs and clasped it around one of his wrists.

"I don't get it—" he said.

"Shh," I said and pulled him by the short chain to the bedroom.

Chapter Four

My heart beat at a wild cadence as Patrick followed my lead into the bedroom. I flicked on the ceiling fan to stir the sweltering air. I didn't look back at him, afraid I'd lose the focus, and the courage to continue. Moonlight filtered in through the tall rectangular window and illuminated our path. The blue hue added an atmospheric component to this surreal moment.

I stacked a couple of pillows at the head of the bed and stood out of his reach as he obediently sat and reclined. He made my bed look small. I'd been alone for so long, and then suddenly I wasn't. I hesitated as my plan of seduction became riddled with doubt. I felt like a fool for trying to pull this off. I drifted back a step, and my mind raced for an escape from this self-inflicted humiliation.

Patrick propped himself onto an elbow.

"I'm sorry," I uttered. "I'll unlock the handcuffs."

"I want you, June," Patrick said. "Anyway. Anyhow."

I moved no farther. He wanted me. Trusted me. What cop would allow this? And he was here for me in any way I chose. I'd never been attracted to anyone more. Maybe the drama from this evening contributed to my heightened feelings and desire, but I didn't care. Was I behaving irrationally? It didn't matter. I didn't want to assess my thoughts and actions anymore. Maybe tomorrow, because tonight I wanted to feel.

My hands trembled as I guided Patrick's arms over his head and cuffed his wrists to the open-frame iron headboard. Secured, he couldn't touch me, and if he couldn't touch me, he wouldn't be able to hurt me. We were distanced just enough for my heart to not be fully engulfed in the fire of love, which could burn so hot and scorch so painfully.

In the celestial light, he looked at me. He didn't say a word. He no doubt found himself in uncertain territory. But then again, so did I.

I unbuttoned his shirt, and my pulse sped up. I'd never undressed a man before. When I finished unfastening them all, I pulled his shirt open and exposed his defined chest and flat, taut abdomen. All the time I'd known him, I did not know the physical perfection he'd been hiding.

I trailed a hand across his chest, down his midriff, and lower to the area where his pants confined him. A throaty sound escaped from his mouth as he pressed back into the pillow.

Rational thoughts receded as sensory receptors amplified. My core became molten. Basic carnal need took control of my body and mind. I undid his belt. He arched to allow me to lower his trousers. My breath caught. In the blue shadows, I boldly removed my top and tossed it aside and then shimmied out of my pants. From under heavy lids, he watched. I'd never been this immodest, brazenly undressing in front of anyone, let alone a man I'd never been intimate with before.

"You're so beautiful," Patrick said.

I knew I wasn't, but I believed Patrick meant what

he said. Maybe I possessed some quality he found alluring. His attraction for me acted like a mountain of kindling, and I was about to combust.

One at a time, I slid my bra straps over my shoulders and unhooked the band. Goose bumps tightened my skin. Patrick's lips parted, but he said nothing. I slid off my panties, withdrawing the final shred of cloth between my body and Patrick's unwavering gaze.

I climbed onto the bed and measuredly straddled his waist.

"June," he whispered and moved his arms, only to be stopped by the constraining cuffs.

I plunged forward to kiss him, and my nipples tingled as they swept his chest. A sound escaped my lips before his mouth devoured mine. Fierce, hard. His tongue dipped and swirled as if starved. His need competed with mine. I grabbed the top bar of the headboard, my body millimeters from Patrick's face. He yanked his arms forward forcefully, and the loud clang of metal startled me. He remained secure, confined.

"Take these off," he said softly, yet pleading with urgency.

I shook my head.

He leaned forward. His tongue swirled and teased. I closed my eyes and became completely engulfed by the sensations Patrick created. The overhead fan circulated air caresses over my damp skin. I shivered. Our lips met again in the most passionate fusion. I didn't want this to end. The full contact of our bodies defined carnal heaven. Nothing could replicate human texture, not silk, velvet, or suede. Currents of intense desire intensified. Poker hot with the need to be quenched. I lowered over him. The gradual entry sparked even more pathways of sensation. Patrick arched upward. I moved steadily, rhythmically, and snapped my head back when tight coils released. My breathing became ragged. Metal rattled as Patrick leaned forward and kissed my neck. I resumed a pace, and Patrick met my rhythm. I caught another wave and shuddered with blinding sparks. Patrick's body tensed and then eased into the comforter. He stopped struggling against his restraints.

He licked his lips. "Damn, you're hot," he said in a low voice.

I brushed my lips over his. "You are," I said quietly, understating what I really felt. Simply put, Patrick was all male. The manliest male. The restrained alpha that still dominated my senses. I dropped to his side and placed a hand on his chest. His heart beat strong. I trailed my fingers along his toned midsection and then lower. I couldn't stop myself.

This baffling evening had yet to complete its finale.

Chapter Five

Bed sheets rustled and brushed over my nakedness as I rolled onto my back. I opened my eyes after a night of minimal sleep and realized I was alone in bed. I had, after all, "mercifully" uncuffed Patrick before we crashed. I grabbed a pillow and put it over my face.

Patrick seemed agreeable last night, but in the next-morning perspective, what did he really think of the kinky bondage? It had been a first for me. How had I become so insatiable? Had my dry spell lasted too long, or had Patrick become too irresistible?

There was a thump at the front door. I tossed the pillow aside and sat up to listen. Floorboards creaked, and I scurried to the closet to grab a robe. I padded barefoot toward sounds in the kitchen.

Dressed in a white T-shirt, and black sweatpants, Patrick took two plates from the cupboard. No matter what he wore, or didn't wear, he affected my sinus rhythm. I tightened my sash, self-conscious in the daylight because of my behavior in the night.

"Good morning," I said and smoothed back some of my tousled hair.

"Yes, it is. I hope I didn't wake you." His face brightened with a smile, and he swooped in for a kiss. "How are you feeling?"

"Really well," I said, elated his apparent happiness

perhaps had something to do with me. "I'm fantastic, actually."

"I took your apartment keys and stepped out to pick up breakfast. I hope you don't mind."

"Of course not."

"Juice?" he asked and handed me a cup with a straw.

"Thanks." I took a sip. "Mm, good. I must be dehydrated."

His mouth turned up.

"The apartment was a sauna last night." My voice trailed off.

The Saturday newspaper sat on the kitchen table, along with a brown paper bag and a cardboard drink tray holding two cups. "Whatcha get?"

"I didn't know your preference, so I got a couple of breakfast sandwiches—one sausage and one bacon. Take your pick."

"Both sound delicious," I said and reached into the bag and placed the hot bagel sandwiches onto plates. Traces of awkwardness and modesty dissipated. Time spent with Patrick was effortless. No games. Just him and me being ourselves. We had, after all, been friends for about two years.

"And I got tea for you. Milk only, bag out."

I stopped and glanced at him. How did he know that? I must have mentioned it at some point. "That's perfect, Patrick, thank you." I sat at the table and took a bite of the succulent bacon sandwich. "This is fantastic."

"Glad you like it," he said and sat beside me. His gaze dropped to where my housecoat gaped open. For someone highly articulate, he seemed to be grasping for words. "Last night, I, had no idea you were into that sort of stuff."

Heat rose to my cheeks.

"Usually I can read people, make accurate predictions about behaviors, but I have to say, you surprised me."

I fidgeted with the corner edge of the newspaper. I didn't know what to say because I didn't want to start explaining. Why I did what I did with the handcuffs would probably make no sense to him. If he knew about my emotional struggle, he'd bolt for the door.

"I hope you enjoyed the surprise."

He smiled. "I rarely like surprises, but yours was most welcome. And appreciated."

"I'm glad," I said, relieved, and lowered my gaze.

Bold black letters of a headline caught my attention, and I pulled the newspaper closer. "Oh my God?" I dropped my sandwich onto the plate.

"What is it?"

"This article."

He picked up the paper and started reading out loud.
Woman Sues Hospital for Malpractice

Eight patients were treated incorrectly for breast cancer, one of whom has stepped forward to press charges against St. Eugene's Hospital and the lab technologist allegedly responsible for the incorrect result.

The hospital CEO wants to assure the public that standard procedure is being strictly followed and lab results can be trusted with confidence. However, he would not comment about the alleged errors. No names are being released at this time.

Patrick put the paper down. "Wow. Were you involved in this when you worked there?"

"You can say that. I was the whistleblower."

"Babe, this is huge." He rubbed his chin. "No wonder you didn't want to go to St. Eugene's last night. I'm really sorry."

But that was only half of the reason I didn't want to go to St. Eugene's last night. "You have nothing to be sorry for."

"How are you coping?"

"Fine. Now. But—"

"But what?"

"Last night, at St. Eugene's, do you remember the woman we saw on our way out?"

"Yes, Victoria? Wait, did she have anything to do with it?" he asked.

My chest tightened. I stared transfixed at the newsprint as memories resurfaced.

"It's her, the one you blew the whistle on, isn't it?" Patrick said. "Damn."

"After reporting her, they bullied me in ways I couldn't have imagined. I was in constant fear, always watching my back."

Patrick placed a hand on mine.

"But do you know what the worst part was? Friends who didn't speak up. I know I had done the right thing, but I'd become ostracized."

"Hey, I know you had a tough go of things back then but if it wasn't for you, more people would have been hurt. You saved lives. You, June Harber, are a hero."

I rested my head on his shoulder. "I've been called a lot of names, but never that." I inhaled his fresh citrus scent. "Thanks for the kind words."

Kind words were still just words.

I'd heard kind words before from someone I had loved and trusted. I'd believed his words. But in the end, those words had strung me along to the blindside.

I straightened. "I should get dressed. Thanks again for the food. When you're done, could you see yourself out, please?" I could only guess what Patrick thought. Not that it mattered. The sooner he discovered I was a mess, the better.

Patrick followed me into the bedroom. He wouldn't let me evade him.

"Is everything okay?"

"Yes, fine." I added a reaffirming nod.

"I'm glad," he said. "I'm going to head to the station to access the database for mug shots. The sooner you scan through them, the better. And I'll see if there is an autopsy date set for our victim."

"It's unlikely," I said. "There's a huge backlog in the morgue. And in the lab."

"They're overworking you, aren't they? Utilizing your diligent work ethic." He spoke with concern and reached for my waistband. He pulled me forward, and I couldn't resist.

"Last night was amazing," he whispered. He kissed me and undid my sash. The knot had seemed to melt away. His hands slipped to my waist and then to the small of my back. He pulled me closer.

"Patrick," I whispered.

"I'm sorry I took advantage of you last night. After what you've been through, I should have let you to rest."

"As I recall, you had no choice in the matter, not unless your name is Harry Houdini."

He chuckled. "May I come by later with those mug shots? Sorry about the rush, but the forgetting-curve timeline is steep. Meanwhile, would you be able to jot down the sequence of yesterday's events and any details you remember, even if you don't think they're significant?"

"Yes, I'll try."

He kissed me on the forehead, too tenderly. I didn't deserve it.

"Try to get some rest. Keep hydrated. I can bring you an aloe drink, or would you like some Gatorade?"

"I'm fine." He showed endearing qualities, and I couldn't help but smile. "Officer Patrick, I never knew you were the doting type."

He stopped, and the corner of his mouth turned up. "Neither did I."

****

After Patrick left, I stepped in the shower. Absorbed in thought, I closed my eyes. The sound of rushing water filled my ears, and I stood in disbelief about everything that had happened in the last twelve hours. Crime scene. Murder. Patrick. I had lived a safe, quiet, celibate existence for two years and BAM, complete upheaval. Shit. But this was all so damn exhilarating. Something sparked to life within me. I had been dulled inside for so long.

I decided to fully commit to help find the murderer. At times like this, I wished I had a superpower. I hated people hurting other people. As for my escapade with Patrick, on his part, I suspect this whole thing could have been ultimately about the chase, not the catch. But if Patrick and I continued our relationship, it would have to be on my "unique" terms.

The water cooled, and I finished rinsing. After drying off, I slipped on a navy boat-neck cotton dress. In line with my Saturday routine, I tidied the place, dusted, and vacuumed. Way past lunch hour, I finished left-over quinoa salad and then made myself another tea. I grabbed a spiral bound notepad and pen and sat on the couch.

As per Patrick's instructions, I wrote yesterday's sequence of events as I remembered them. Everything had happened so quickly, and the scant parts of my memory already had too many holes. I thought, and I thought. I had seen the crook's profile, but nothing stood out. No remarkable nose. No tattoos or beard that I could remember. Just a Caucasian guy in his twenties or early thirties. I dropped the pen and paper onto the coffee table and sipped my now lukewarm tea. Disgusted with both the tea, and myself, I put the mug down. I would not be much help.

A loud knock cut through the quiet. I looked through the sheer curtain and saw Patrick with a black satchel hanging over his shoulder. He held a tray with two beverages. I cracked a smile, hurried to the door, and swung it open.

Patrick had changed into a red plaid shirt, black jeans, and rustic brown boots. His eyes were as blue as a deep ocean. I tried to act unaffected and professional while thoughts of the night before intruded. As observant as he was, I hoped he wouldn't see the pulse beating wildly at my jugular. I had to stop this visceral reaction. I reasoned this was simply an evolutionary response— like a cave woman wanting to breed with the strongest male to ensure the survival of the species. I had to focus. We had work to do.

We both said, "Hi." He seemed at a loss for words as well, like a shy schoolboy. He stepped onto the entrance mat, and I shut the door behind him. He started removing his boots, and I reached for the drink tray. "Here, let me take that."

"Oh, thanks." He placed his boots beside the bench.

"I thought we could sit in here," I said and motioned to the living room. The wood floor creaked under our socked feet as we shuffled into the next room. I couldn't lie. Things felt a little awkward right now. After having unleashed the beast, so to speak, the night before, once again I felt a little self-conscious.

Patrick sat on the couch at the front window and removed a laptop from his satchel. I put the drinks on the coffee table and picked up my mug of cold tea. "I'm just going to get rid of this."

"Yes, sure," he said and started typing.

I hurried into the kitchen and dumped the old tea into the sink. I glanced around and opened a cupboard while looking for some food to nibble on. I grabbed a half-eaten jar of peanuts and put it down. No nuts.

I rejoined Patrick and sat beside him. The inhalation of his fresh scent seemed to increase my mental clarity, ease the tension, and warm my insides. If there was a thermal image scan of my body, I knew what areas would glow redder by the second. I inwardly groaned and pulled the fabric of the front of my dress up to cover my nose.

"Are you all right?" He stopped working as he waited for my answer.

I let the fabric go, and the neck of my dress line slipped back into place. "I'm fine, well better than fine. I'm good. Really good." I hoped Patrick knew me well enough to know I wasn't as dumb as I just sounded.

He grinned. "I'm glad." He put the laptop on the coffee table. "So, I've set this up for you. I adjusted the demographics to white males, ages eighteen to fifty. Scroll through them. Take your time. If you see any guy that looks familiar, just click on it, and we can come back to it."

"All right. I think I can handle that." I started scrolling on the touchpad, and he handed me a nice warm cup. "Oh, thank you," I said and sipped tea as I looked at one solemn face after another. After examining several more, I shook my head. "No luck yet."

"Take your time," he said and slipped a hand to the nape of my neck and massaged gently. Goose bumps tingled and rippled from the focal point of his touch. My thoughts drifted to last night when Patrick and I were in bed. And then I realized I wasn't paying adequate attention to the faces scrolling across the display. I moved forward and perched on the edge of the couch and pretended to concentrate more intently on the screen. Patrick's hand dropped away, but my desire remained ignited.

I scrolled back to revisit the faces I hadn't paid complete attention to.

Patrick took the plastic lid off his paper cup and took a drink. "Someone look familiar?"

"Maybe," I fibbed. I started chewing on the side of my thumbnail. His closeness made it impossible for me to focus.

Patrick leaned forward. "Is this too difficult for you? We can take a break."

I coughed, choking for a second, and then almost laughed. "No, I'm fine. I can absolutely keep going. We have to find this guy no matter what." I kept looking. I searched through the long list once, and then again. Nothing registered familiar, nothing emerged from the recesses of my memory. "God dammit," I said under my breath. "I really suck at this."

His arms reached around me and cradled me against his chest. His cheek brushed mine. I fully inhaled his scent. His possessive arms held me firm.

"Don't be so hard on yourself. You're an excellent witness. Thanks to you we have a lead in the case." In circular motions, he swirled his fingers on the fabric of my dress at my midsection. He had touched no intimate areas, yet they heated nonetheless. The embers were getting hotter. If his hand moved any higher or lower, there'd be combustion. My breathing became irregular, even more so as he kissed my neck.

"Oh my God," I whispered. I quivered. His lips covered mine perfectly. How was that even possible? His hand wandered out of the circle and moved upward.

Ignition.

With great effort, I pushed away. "Patrick," I said and adjusted my dress and hair. Not really caring how I looked, it was merely an attempt to regain self-control.

Passion glistened in his eyes, and his lips remained parted. "Sorry. I didn't mean to take advant—"

"You didn't. There's just work to be done."

He nodded. "There is."

The problem was that I couldn't convince my body and mind to focus on anything other than Patrick. It was futile. Cutting off reason, I turned and practically leapt into his lap. I straddled Patrick's thighs, wrapped my arms around his neck, and locked his lips to mine. His hands cupped my rear and held me close. I unbuttoned his shirt and ran my hands along his firm torso.

"I love your fingers," he whispered. "But you touched me, inside, long before you used your hands." He leaned forward to reclaim my lips with his, but I didn't engage. I wouldn't let his tantalizing poetic words toy with my mind. They were said in the heat of this moment, and that's all they'd be. Words. I had to remember that.

I moved off his lap, stood, and took a few steps back. The look in his eyes appeared distressed and confused. He stood to follow, but I lifted my index finger.

"Just a second. Wait there."

Obediently, he waited in place. His expression relaxed, and he raised a brow. I scurried into the hallway, opened the closet door, and, from a hanger, grabbed a thin yellow fringed scarf. I held one end and let the other end drag on the floor behind me. With slow, fluid steps, I returned to Patrick. He slipped an arm around my waist and leaned in to kiss me, but his lips missed the mark when I turned my head. I eased his arm from my waist and looped the scarf around his wrist. The corner of his mouth curled, and he let me continue. I stepped behind him and tied both of his wrists together with a firm tug. I moved in front of him. He stood there, statuesque and bound like a felon. But his only crime was trying to steal my heart.

He looked at me more seriously, probably anticipating my next move. Funny, I hadn't planned one yet. His pecs flinched, and I drew in a quick shallow breath. His physicality affected me so acutely I could barely contain myself. Warm magma flowed to my lower region, engulfing, engorging. I undid the top button of Patrick's jeans and slipped them down to his thighs. The fabric of his white briefs strained. I pushed at his firm midsection, and he sat on the sofa with his hands secured behind him.

I lifted my dress enough to resume a straddled position on his lap. He kissed my shoulder, then my collarbone, where the neckline of my dress gaped open. My focus went lower. I fumbled to free him, and he raised his hips to assist. The anticipation alone surged even more neuropeptides through my veins. I kissed Patrick and then pulled away a mere millimeter.

"Are you cool with this?" I whispered.

He leaned forward to continue the dancing of our mouths. I got my answer.

Bound and with no recourse, Patrick nuzzled his face into my clothed chest. Even through the fabric, my chest tingled. I moved aside the narrow panel of my panties and positioned myself. I eased down, and the intense sensations rippled. With my eyes closed, I was oblivious to everything but Patrick. I braced my hands on his shoulders, and, like an equestrian, I posted in rhythm. Spasms exploded, and I let out a small cry. My breathing remained erratic as I continued on the crashing swell. Patrick's chest and shoulders flexed, followed by a sharp tear of fabric.

I slumped onto Patrick and rested my cheek on his shoulder, lulled by the rise and fall of his chest. I lingered in our calm intimacy. Like the sun at dusk, the afterglow gradually set. The pulsing at his carotid slowed, and I moved to look at him. A grin widened across his lips, and he brought his once-bound hands forward. He held the ripped scarf in one hand, and I laughed.

"Sorry about this." He chuckled. "I guess you should have used the handcuffs."

Chapter Six

"Thanks, bud," Patrick said and shut the door, holding a paper bag of Chinese food.

"Want to eat on the sofa?" I said. "Maybe there's a movie on TV."

"Sure, sounds good." He sat and unpacked the cardboard food boxes one by one and put them on the coffee table. "We've got orange beef, stir-fry, Szechuan noodles, chicken, and here's the steamed rice."

"Smells amazing," I said and watched him dig in. It seemed unbelievable how my life had changed in forty-eight hours. And it was because of him. Officer Patrick Verbeek. How had he punched holes in my walls? Could I trust him to break them down completely?

No.

Not yet.

I turned on the television and clicked through several channels. "Here. How about this?"

"Gladiators? You know what a guy likes, don't you?"

I smiled and lowered my eyes.

Minutes into the film, blood splattered as characters fought to their gruesome deaths.

Patrick dipped a breaded chicken ball into the bright red sweet and sour sauce. "Maybe this wasn't the best choice of film."

I laughed. "I'm sure we can handle it."

A memory popped into my head. "Patrick, I remember something."

"What is it?" He turned down the volume.

"The guy that knocked me into the dumpster looked back at me before he ran away. I can't pinpoint the exact details of his face, but I remember he had something red at the side of his eye. Like a scratch or a cut. His face may have been swollen too." My joy was short-lived because that was all I could remember. I got a sinking feeling. My great revelation did nothing to help identify him. "Sorry, that's all I got."

Patrick put down his plate. "No. That's good. We now know he took some punches. The more information we have about him, the better. We have his DNA, and hopefully he'll be in the database."

There were a few bites of food left on my plate, but I had had enough. I placed my dish on the table.

"June?" He didn't continue speaking until I looked at him. "We're going to get him." The assured tone in his voice left no doubt in my mind. I eased back onto the couch. He put his arm around me, and I snuggled close as we watched the film. Before long, the end credits started rolling.

"I hate to say this, but I should go," he said. "I have to stop at the station."

I sat up and tried to ignore the ping of disappointment. But it was for the best. I couldn't let myself get attached.

I held Patrick's hand as we walked onto the porch and into the refreshing night air. I thought he was going to draw me into his arms for a farewell kiss, but he glared toward the road.

"Get inside, June," he said in a stiff tone. A dark car parked behind mine, with someone sitting at the wheel. The driver pulled around my car, almost clipping it, and screeched away. Patrick dashed to the curb, and I followed. The air stunk of exhaust. He turned and gave me a disapproving shake of his head.

"Could you make out anything?" I said, pretending to ignore his scolding expression.

"No. I couldn't get a good look at the driver through the tinted windows. I think it was a male," he said and charged over to his pickup truck. From inside, he grabbed a flashlight and searched the road and sidewalk for any clues. Nothing. He turned to me. "Come on. Let's go inside."

Patrick insisted on looking around in the backyard, walking through my duplex apartment, and checking the locks.

"Do you want me to stay the night? I can return in a couple of hours," he said. With furrowed brows, he looked worried.

"Patrick, do you really think the person in that car had anything to do with me? He probably pulled over to talk to a girlfriend and took off when he saw us."

"You were at a murder scene, June. Don't be dismissive."

"I was at a murder scene, sure, but who saw me? The bad guy knocked me from behind and ran away. Right?"

Patrick nodded. "Perhaps. But just in case, make sure you don't open your door for anyone." He slid his arms around me.

He showed he cared, and I reveled in holding him close. "Yes, Officer, I can do that."

"But will you?"

"I can. And I will."

"Good. And keep your outdoor lights on." He swooped in for a kiss. "I can't get enough of you, June Harber."

I knew what he meant.

"Call 911 if you hear or see anything. Want me to enter it into your speed dial?"

I laughed and smacked his rear before he scooted to his truck.

Chapter Seven

Monday morning, I zipped into the last parking spot at work. Pressed for time, I didn't straighten my car to fit nicely between the lines. I grabbed my travel mug, handbag, and scurried across the parking lot. My heels clicked like trotting pony hooves. I rummaged through my purse for my ID badge but couldn't find it, so I pressed the buzzer beside the door.

"Forensics," a familiar male voice said from the speaker.

"Hey, Charlie, it's June. I forgot my badge; can you buzz me in?"

"Wow, that's a first. No problem." The latch clicked.

"Thank you!" I rushed down the hall, dumped my stuff in the locker room, and entered the lab. The door slammed behind me, and I blew hair from my eyes. My three co-workers remained motionless, staring at me.

"Good morning," I said. Still, no one moved. "What's up?" I asked and reached for my hung-up lab coat.

Edward Ying finally moved; the more-salt-than-pepper-haired DNA guru put down a tray of samples. "You're late. And your hair's down. Are you sick?"

I buttoned my coat. "I'm not sick. And it's five to eight. Technically, I'm early."

Lara Lambert shuffled papers on the bench top. "For you, this is late." She spoke with a French accent, having emigrated from Brussels only eight years ago. She moved toward me and looked down. "You're wearing a skirt. And pumps."

I pulled on a pair of gloves and went to the fridge to retrieve my samples. "You wear a skirt and heels every day, Lara." I didn't want to add she also wore pantyhose, even in ninety-degree weather.

Lara nodded. "Yes, I do, but you don't. You wear pajamas, I mean, scrubs."

The others snickered.

I shook my head as I lined up my specimens. "Will you guys stop already? So, I dressed up a bit. Big deal." I went to the locked fridge to search for the items Patrick said he had dropped off. I turned to Vinny Fuller, the most senior analyst. He sat beside me on a tall stool, logging in forensic evidentiary items including cigarette butts, torn fabric, and a toothbrush.

"Hey, Vinny," I said. "Have you come across any recent items such as bloody gauze in a jar, or maybe a knife from a crime scene?"

Vinny scrunched his nose and pushed up his black-framed glasses. His magnified eyes showed surprise, and then he scratched his bald head. "Actually, yes. Those exact items are waiting to be processed. How did you know about them?" He leaned closer to me. "What's that black stuff around your eyes?" he said and then chuckled like a hyena.

I broke down and finally laughed at all the razzing. "Okay, guys, it's getting old. Now, let's get some work done, shall we?" I focused on my tasks when I heard the door open and close.

"Good morning, Officer Verbeek," Edward Ying said. "What brings you here this morning?"

Heavy police boots walked across the room toward me. My heart skipped.

"Good morning. I'm here to speak with June," Patrick said in the strong, deep voice that struck a tender part inside of me, especially when he uttered my name. He stood an arm's length away, clean shaven and dapper in his crisp uniform.

I angled away from Patrick, then glanced at my co-workers. All eyes were on us. Lara cracked a smile, and Edward gave me a thumbs-up behind Patrick's back.

My cheeks burned, and I inwardly groaned. I tried to act nonchalant so the others wouldn't figure out Patrick and I were a thing. But I had a feeling they'd already figured out our secret. No one could hide anything from this team of experts.

"Good morning, Officer Verbeek," I said, keeping it formal. But Patrick's knowing gaze and his hand on my lower back showed our relationship had evolved into something much less formal.

"You look hot as hell," he whispered.

I tried not to smile. Everyone's attention was still on us. All they needed was movie popcorn and a fountain drink to make their viewing experience more enjoyable.

"How's everyone?" Patrick said, glancing around, facing their stares full on. I wished I could be as cool and calm as Patrick appeared to be. No doubt my blushing cheeks were turning shades of red.

"Is that a rhetorical question, Officer?" Vinny said. "Cause if you really want to know how we're doing, you better have a seat."

Patrick chuckled and sat on a stool. "Still a huge

backlog?"

I couldn't help smiling. Patrick's personable gesture showed he cared about everyone.

"Oh, yes. Weeks' worth of backlog," Lara said. "So don't bring us any more. Not to mention our genetic analyzer is almost caput, and reagents are on back order. Which wouldn't have been so bad if somebody hadn't knocked over a bottle of gel-loading solution." She gave Vinny the evil eye.

"It's not my intention to increase your workload, trust me," Patrick said. "But I have a murder victim slated for an autopsy. What's the probability of that being done today?"

"You mean the probability of it being done this month, don't you?" Edward said. "And that's only if the new pathologist shows up."

"We're getting a new pathologist?" I said, louder than I intended. Everyone looked over, and I shrugged in the awkward moment. "Sorry, I didn't know we got approval."

"Well, that's great news, right?" Patrick said.

"It is," Vinny said. "But we also need to hire a new lab tech. June thrives on the overtime, but I personally don't want any extra hours."

I shrugged again. "I wouldn't exactly say I thrive on it."

Patrick winked at me. "Have you begun analysis of the most recent items I brought in?"

I shook my head, then blew at the insistent hair falling in my eyes. "No, actually, I just got in."

Vinny laughed in the background, most certainly about my "lateness."

"June, may I speak with you in private for a

moment?" Patrick asked.

"Of course." I followed him out of the lab and into the hallway, away from all the inquisitive ears.

He looked at me intensely. "Are you all right?" he said. "Are you feeling any post-traumatic stress?"

I rubbed my forehead. "I don't think so. Maybe. Maybe not." I leaned against the wall. "I think you've affected me more than the guy who body checked me into the dumpster."

Patrick moved closer, but then stepped back when a door slammed down the hall. Footsteps and the sound of jingling keys approached. It was Charlie, the security guard.

"Good morning," he said. He held his stocky form in straight posture. It was obvious he hit the gym regularly—a deterrent to mess with him right off the bat.

Patrick and I greeted him.

Charlie walked past us and then turned. "June, do you need a temporary badge 'til you find yours?"

"Yeah, that'd be great. I can stop by security later to pick it up."

Charlie waved, then stepped outside to do his usual security checks of the building's perimeter.

"You can't find your badge?" Patrick asked.

"No, I must have left it at home. I've been a bit distracted lately."

"As have I," he whispered and moved closer.

I lowered my gaze and noticed the shiny silver badge on his chest. I felt the blood drain from my face. Panic fizzed up in my chest like seltzer.

"What just happened? June?"

"Patrick," I started to say and cleared my constricted throat. "My work badge, it's actually missing."

"Missing? But you said you left it at home."

I put my hand on his chest. "Yes, that's what I thought. But I realized the last time I had my ID badge was when I was attacked."

Patrick clenched his jaw.

"What if the guy who shoved me has my badge? He'd know my name, what I look like, where I work, and have access to this building. He could find out where I live."

"June, I'll speak to Charlie and have him deactivate your badge."

"Okay, good," I said and wrung my hands.

"We'll take every precaution to keep you safe."

His comfort was immeasurable. I could see concern on his face, but I didn't know if he was worried about my state of upset, or about the potential escalated danger of the case. Probably both. From the beginning, he took my involvement in the case seriously, and I wished I hadn't downplayed it. I shivered.

"Thank you, Patrick."

He gently kissed the top of my head.

I pulled my shoulders back and focused on my mission.

I had work to do to help solve this mystery.

Chapter Eight

I marched into the lab. With the possible threat of a criminal knowing my identity and workplace, analyzing the blood sample Patrick had swabbed off my arm became top priority.

I had to enlighten my colleagues about my situation.

Vinny looked up from his computer monitor as I rooted myself in the center of the lab. Lara shut the centrifuge lid and glanced over and then nudged Edward with an elbow, who sat beside her.

"Hey, guys," I said. "I have something to tell all of you, something you should know, for your own safety."

"Safety?" Vinny stood, wide-eyed. "I knew it. They're real, aren't they?"

"What's real?" I asked, with no idea of what he was talking about.

Lara rolled her eyes. "Aliens. Vinny's referring to aliens."

"Like extraterrestrial aliens?" I shook my head. "Gosh, I don't know if they're real."

"You don't? You mean you weren't abducted?" Vinny said and scratched his bald head. "But there were so many signs."

Edward snorted. "Get real, Vinny."

"He is real," Lara said. "He honestly believes little green men exist. Says he has proof—bacteria from the clouds of Venus, or something."

"Shhh! Not so loud," Vinny said.

Lara waved him off. "What is it, June? What's going on."

I took a breath. "Last Friday, I missed my bus, and Officer Verbeek was kind enough to offer me a ride home."

The others exchanged glances.

"On the way, we stopped at a disturbance call that turned out to be a murder scene, and the apparent perp shoved me into a dumpster, and now my work badge is missing."

Dead silence.

"Dear God, June." Lara ran over and hugged me. "You poor thing. Are you all right?"

"I'm fine. But if we assume this person has my badge and knows where I work, we should all be on the lookout for anything suspicious. Maybe use the buddy system when going to our vehicles."

"I have mace," Lara said with excitement. "And my spiked heels are an excellent weapon."

"Good stuff," Vinny said. "I can fill syringes of etorphine for all of us to carry."

I giggled. "Vinny, this isn't a TV episode of that vigilante serial killer."

No one else laughed.

"Wait," I said. "You have access to etorphine?"

Vinny pursed his lips and remained silent.

"Okay, guys," I said. "I think it would be best to focus on analyzing the blood swabbed from my arm, the potential murder weapon, and items from the crime scene. The sooner this guy gets caught, the safer we'll all be."

Edward cleared his throat. "Are we all in for overtime tonight, people? I know I am."

Everyone nodded, and tears moistened my eyes. I worked with a considerate bunch. They were a little odd at times, even worrisome, but I couldn't ask for a better group to rely on.

****

I put the automatic pipette down and shook my hand. Without looking at a clock, the aching in my thumb alerted me I'd reached my limit for the day. I inserted the plastic tray of dispensed samples into the analyzer and touched a series of buttons on the screen to start the overnight run. It was now up to the instrument to complete the sequencing.

Tomorrow, DNA analysis would be complete.

At the end of a long shift, we all stood near the sink, waiting for our turn to wash our hands. The phone rang, and I grabbed the receiver beside me.

"Forensics. June Harber."

"Hi, June. How are you doing?" Patrick said.

"Hey, I was just thinking about you. Do you like salmon?" I curled the spiral phone cord around my finger.

"Yes, I do."

"Great, because I have a couple filets in my freezer and I thought I'd bake them for dinner, if you would like to join me."

"Ah, sorry I'd love to, but I've been in court all day and still have work to finish."

My insides sank. "No problem. I can save them for another night."

I tried not to appear disappointed when I hung up. I said good night to my crew, and on the way out I stopped by security and picked up a new ID badge. The wind whipped the door open and then slammed it shut with a deafening bang. Jumbo clouds billowed in a dreary gray sky, and I held my skirt down while battling uplifting gusts.

The heavens became darker by the second. I wanted to get home before the impending downpour but took a detour. Something compelled me to go back to the scene of the crime. Perhaps it was morbid curiosity. Or maybe an investigative inclination. But most likely wishful thinking. I parked directly in front of the house. They sealed off the entire perimeter of the property with yellow police tape.

All seemed motionless and quiet within the confined area. I touched the yellow plastic barrier and debated crawling under. Movement flashed to my left, and I spun around. A woman in a trench coat held a taut leash to her sniffing beagle.

"I wouldn't go in there, dear," she said. "There was a murder last week."

"Really?" I hadn't realized the crime had made the news. "Hi, I'm June. Do you live near here?"

"Mabel. And yes, I live around the corner. I have got to tell you; the neighborhood is mighty nervous after what happened. It's always been such a safe area."

"I can imagine," I said, withholding details about my involvement. "Do you, by any chance, know who lives in this house and who was murdered? Has there been any previous disturbances?"

Her dog lurched. "I have no idea who was murdered. I'm guessing it was over drugs or something. It's a rental, I do know that. People come and go, but without happenstance, unlike now."

The house sat in a foreboding darkness.

The dog dragged the woman forward. "Well, be careful, June," she called out behind her. "You never know who's lurking where. Have a good evening."

"You too," I said. Instead of returning to my car, I walked along the length of the tape. It stopped at the dumpster. I could still envision Patrick racing down the alley after the suspect. Automatically, I turned and headed down the hedge-lined lane and used my phone's torchlight. I scrutinized the dirt and gravel. I didn't know why I was doing this, but maybe it would help jog my memory.

I'd traipsed about a hundred yards and stopped, glancing at the house's unremarkable backyard. Birds flew over my head into a large tree. Or maybe they were bats. Lightning cracked in the black sky. The wind whistled, and the temperature noticeably dropped. I retraced my steps when suddenly a stone jumped into one of my pumps. Balancing on one foot, I took off my shoe and shook out the pebble. My phone somersaulted out of my hand and tumbled to the ground.

Damn.

The light flashed into the hedge, and I noticed a scrap of paper amongst the fallen leaves. I squatted and then dropped to my knees to fetch it. It was a business card. I shone the phone light onto it. The name on the card was Dr. Fulthorpe, Hematologist, St. Eugene's Hospital.

My heart hammered. I turned the card over, and in black ink an address was written—109 Landry Road. This address.

How did this card get here, and whose was it? Could it have belonged to the guy that knocked me down? Or was I grasping?

What really happened there?

Wind tugged at my hair, and thunder cracked. Clouds burst, and heavy rain poured. Wet clothes clung to my body, and I pushed dripping hair from my eyes. My heels sunk into the wet earth as I sprinted to my car. The smooth soles of my shoes held no traction, and I slipped on the slick grass and fell onto my rear. I scrambled to my feet and shuffled the rest of the way, sloshing into a puddle on the road before climbing into my car. Saturated, cold, and mucky, I sat inside my vehicle. I put the dirty, wet business card onto the seat beside me and panted.

What the hell was I doing? I felt like an idiot, probably looked like one too, searching for clues in an electrical storm. They did not train me in this field of investigation.

I turned on the ignition and looked at the house and at the dumpster. Shivering, I flipped on the heat.

Yes, I was inexperienced in crime investigation. Green as an Irish meadow. But, with my safety at risk, I was even more motivated to learn pretty damn quick.

Chapter Nine

I slammed the car door and darted through the rain into my apartment. In the doorway, I removed my mud-caked shoes, torn stockings, and soiled sweater and dress. I ambled to the bedroom closet and put on a robe and a pair of flip-flop slippers. With an armful of soiled clothes, I headed out the back door and descended the exterior stairs to the basement laundry room. Debra, the upstairs tenant, and I shared the washer and dryer down cellar, which was only accessible by a separate exterior entrance. Fortunately, an awning covered the outside staircase.

The old unfinished cellar housed spiders and centipedes of exceptional size, and I never knew when I'd find a flooded floor from the sewer backup. I grabbed the key from under the mat and realized I didn't need it. I pushed open the unlatched door—Debra often left it unlocked. I flipped on the switch to the dangling bulb, but the light didn't turn on.

Great.

In the darkness, I headed to the washer. A dehumidifier rattled on the other side of the room. I tried to ignore the eerie storage area filled with dusty stacks of boxes, random house items, and even a creepy dress form.

I strained to see as I opened the lid of the washer and

dropped in my clothes with a detergent pod. I hit buttons, and the machine rumbled to life. I turned to head back upstairs when a gust of air blew across my face and tickled my neck. I froze. I tried not to think of the fact that I believed in ghosts. Cool air continued to circulate around me, and goose bumps covered my forearms. The basement window gaped open. I reached up to shut it and brushed my hand through a sticky web. I gasped, busted outside, and darted up the stairs as fast as I could.

I hated that old creepy basement.

My chest heaved, and I locked the back door. With everything that had been happening the past few days, my nerves were fraying. I could almost feel them, popping one fiber at a time. I wondered why the basement window was open. The most obvious reason dawned on me, which was that someone had tried to break in. Or maybe someone had broken in. Or maybe someone had broken in and was still in the basement. My legs felt like jelly, and I dove for my cell phone. I called Patrick's number, but it went to voicemail.

"Hey, Patrick, it's me. Please call me. Thanks."

I tiptoed through the apartment and surveyed each room and closet. Nothing appeared to be touched or disturbed. I relaxed a smidgen.

A forceful knock sounded at the front door, and I dropped behind the couch to hide from view. My heart thumped like the dribbling of a basketball. There was another loud knock. I didn't move as I waited for whoever it was to go away.

I fumbled with my phone when I heard a man's voice from outside.

"June! Are you in there?"

Patrick. I wanted to cry with relief. "Just a second."

I scrambled up from my crouched position and opened the door. Still in uniform, Patrick stepped inside from the foyer. I followed his gaze to my black bra, where my housecoat gaped open. Patrick raised his eyebrows, and the corner of his mouth turned up.

"Hi," I said and shrugged my shoulders. I tried to smile, but a sob tore out of my chest. I couldn't talk.

Patrick kicked the door shut and plunged toward me. "Hey. What's wrong?"

My body shook. "Sorry. Just freaking out a bit here."

"Why? What happened?"

"It's probably nothing, but I found the basement window open."

"Show me."

I paused at the threshold of the back door and stared out into the glistening wet darkness. I couldn't move.

Patrick pulled the gun from his hip. "Lock yourself in the bathroom, June."

In a flash, he disappeared down the stairwell.

I listened for any sound from below. There was a crash and then nothing. I couldn't stand there like a frozen scaredy-cat, so I grabbed the biggest knife from the knife block. I descended the steps, my thighs shaky with each step. I opened the basement door. Moonglow drifted in, but I didn't see Patrick.

"Patrick?" I whispered.

At the back of the room, something shifted in the darkness, and then a beam of light flared. Patrick appeared from behind the storage pile with a flashlight.

"It's okay, June. I'm here," he said.

"Did you find anything?"

"I don't want to alarm you, but there was definitely

someone down here. I already called it in."

"Oh." My stomach clenched.

"Have a look," he said and went over to the hanging light bulb. He rotated it farther into the socket, and it lit up. "It appears someone loosened it. We'll have to check it for prints, as well as the door and window. It looks like they jimmied the window open, and there are some muddy footprints."

I squeezed the shaft of the knife.

Patrick looked at my clinched hand. "Way to hustle, darling."

I choked out a laugh. "How do you do this sort of stuff all the time without heart failure?"

"Training, experience," he said. "How about we get out of here?"

Patrick followed close behind me as we climbed the stairs and reentered my apartment. I slid the knife back into the wooden block and clasped my hands together to steady them.

"The thought of a stranger being down there is unnerving. I can't shake it," I said. "I wish I could be as brave and calm as you. You're really incredible. You can think when there's danger, you're adept and—"

"June, don't idolize me."

It took me aback how he accepted no accolades. He was humble, or perhaps at one time had been humbled.

He took my hand and led me to the couch. I nestled against him. He stroked my back, and I closed my eyes. His closeness and warmth were like a secure hammock. I loved the strength of his mind and body.

"June?"

I opened my eyes and sat up. Lights flashed outside.

"The detectives arrived. Will you be okay staying

here alone while I assist downstairs?"

Tears stung my eyes.

Worry crinkled Patrick's brow, and he put an arm around me. "You're shaking."

"Sorry," I whispered. My fear multiplied, irrationally.

"June, I want you to stay at my place tonight. Would that be okay with you?"

I nodded, relieved I'd be somewhere that felt safe. But would anywhere be safe until we solved this case?

"Patrick? Can I ask you a favor?"

"Of course."

"Would you mind taking me shopping sometime?"

"Yes, absolutely. Need a dose of retail therapy?" He smiled. "What do you want to buy?"

I glanced at his belt and then back up at him.

"A gun."

Chapter Ten

From the closet and dresser drawers, I made quick selections and crammed a few days' worth of clothes into a duffle bag I wished was bigger. On top, I squeezed in a small tote of toiletries.

I stepped out into the mild evening air. Patrick finished speaking with two detectives and then jogged over and took my bag.

"So, how do you want to do this? Do you want to follow me in your car?"

"That'll work."

He put my bag into the trunk of my car and, as a gentleman, opened the door to seat me inside. He then got into his cruiser.

I put the key into the ignition and turned it. The engine started fine, but then a knocking sounded under the hood. Patrick pulled away, and I shifted into drive. I tapped the gas, but the engine sputtered and shut off. I turned the key, but my car wouldn't start up again. Patrick parked and got out.

"It died," I said.

He tried to start the motor, but without success. "Have you had previous engine trouble?"

"No, none."

"It's getting late. Do you want to drive with me, and we can send for a tow tomorrow?"

"Okay," I said, realizing there wasn't much choice in the matter. My insides sunk. Had my old reliable car seen its last days?

We retrieved my bag from the trunk and then got into Patrick's squad car.

He smiled. "Let's try this again."

I appreciated his attempt to put me at ease with his kind disposition, though the post break-in feeling of violation still lingered. "So, what did you and the detectives do in the basement?"

"We looked around, snapped some shots, and lifted a few prints and a partial shoe tread."

Patrick scanned the streets as he drove. We talked a little more. He reached over and put a reassuring hand on my knee. No touch of his was lost on me. Its warmth helped dissipate my anxiousness.

We drove down a country road. Perhaps ten miles out, Patrick turned onto a driveway and parked in front of a ranch farmhouse. He guided me out of the car and carried my bag up the walkway.

"Watch your footing. I've been meaning to fix some loose flagstones."

"Patrick, I appreciate everything you're doing for me," I said and noticed how weary my voice sounded.

He stopped. "Of course. I'm here for you, babe." The country night sky was like a black abyss dotted with countless stars, and I realized I heard chirping crickets for the first time in a long time. A subtle tranquility flowed through me as I inhaled clean air and earthen smells.

Patrick let me into the house and flicked on the light.

"Welcome to my humble abode," he said and placed my bag on the bench.

"Thank you for having me." I admired the wood interior, high ceilings, and overhead beams. I took off my shoes and put them on the weaved mat.

We walked on weathered pine flooring into the living area with a tan sectional sofa. A folded afghan was draped on the backrest. My toes sunk into the soft jute area rug as I waited for Patrick to turn on brass floor lamps. A rich wooden staircase and railing spiraled up to a loft.

He followed the direction of my gaze. "My bedroom is up there, in the loft."

"It's lovely here, Patrick."

"Thank you. Please, make yourself at home."

I sat and tucked my feet under me and put an elbow on the armrest. I watched Patrick with captivation. He crouched at a natural stone fireplace with masonry up to the high ceiling. A sheet at a time, he crumpled newspaper and crammed them under the grate. He added kindling and a couple of logs and struck a long match, igniting several areas of the paper. Almost immediately, flames were ablaze. Patrick continued pushing scrunched paper under the grate with a wrought iron poker until all the wood burned.

"Would you like some wine? Or some brandy to warm you?"

His attentiveness had already warmed me.

"I wouldn't mind a splash of brandy." I didn't understand why I had asked for something I'd never drunk before.

"I'll be right back."

The flames mesmerized and lulled. I gravitated to the stone hearth. The heat soothed my soul, and stressful thoughts faded. Patrick joined me with two glasses of amber fluid. He held one out for me and the reflection of the fire danced in the liquid.

"I'd been saving this Remy Martin. Won it at a stag after a fierce coin toss competition." He chuckled.

I carefully took the glass from him, feeling a little tipsy already. He sat beside me and rested his forearms on his knees. He swirled his drink. Unexplainably, his mere presence calmed me, grounded me, assured me. "Thank you for bringing me here," I said.

"I won't rest until we figure out what is happening. I don't want you to be afraid."

I shook my head. "I'm not afraid. Not now." I believed every word he said, because I knew he meant them. And I realized I believed everything he said because I trusted him.

"You're brave, June. And you've remained composed after everything you've been through this past week."

"Well, I sure fooled you." I smiled and took a drink of the Remy. Liquid fire ran from my mouth to my belly. I watched Patrick's profile. Without effort, he could overpower me, but all he'd shown was concern, support, and passion. He embodied everything I'd longed for, so why was I still so fearful of letting my guard down?

"As you can see, my place is more or less an open concept. Would you like a tour of the rest of the house?" It took a couple of seconds for my thoughts to recede and Patrick's words to register.

"Hmm. I'd love that," I said.

We placed the empty glasses into the double basin sink. "This is the kitchen and eating area. Obviously."

"That's a lovely table," I said.

"Thank you. It was my grandmother's." He moved

the curtain aside. "It's too dark out, but this window has a view of the rear yard and woods."

I put my nose to the window and saw only blackness. "I can't wait to see your property in daylight. Oh, I think I just saw a pair of eyes."

He chuckled. "You probably did. It could have been a racoon or a skunk. Though coyotes make appearances as well. Don't worry. They won't bother us. Come."

It'd be easy for a person to hide out there, too. I pushed the idea from my mind.

He pointed. "Those stairs lead to the loft, and the en suite." Along the main floor hallway, he opened a door. "This here is a bathroom. And the laundry/mud room is next to it."

"I like the laundry on the main floor," I said.

He listened intently and understood. "Yes, it is. Are you hungry? I can fix you something."

"I'm fine, thank you. You have a beautiful home, Patrick. I really love it."

He smiled. "I hoped you would."

I put a hand to my mouth and stifled a yawn.

"I'll show you upstairs, and we can call it a night."

He grabbed my duffel bag from the hallway, and we climbed the stairs to the loft. On the night table, he turned on a lamp that better illuminated the simple layout. He had a large dresser, a king-size bed, and a television mounted on the wall. The skylight made the room appear more spacious and added a touch of calm with the boundless view.

He put down my luggage. "That door leads to the bathroom."

I sat on the bed and sank into the cushiony-soft black-and-white striped comforter.

"Make yourself comfortable, June. Through the railing you'll have a view of me on the couch below. Holler if you need anything. I'll be listening."

"What?" Had I heard right? "You're going down there to sleep?"

"I know you need your rest, and I don't want to be presumptuous."

How could he think of leaving me now? Downstairs was too far away.

"Wait." I jumped up and stood in front of him. He stood statuesque, powerful, and bronzed in the soft light. "Please stay here." I rested my fingertips on his chest. The more time I spent with him, spoke with him, kissed him, the more I wanted him. I unbuttoned his shirt and slid it over his shoulders. I kissed where my fingers had been, and his chest expanded. He encircled me with his arms. I wanted to break the rule I had created for myself, but I couldn't. Not yet. I reached around and withdrew Patrick's arms.

"June," he breathed. "Tell me what you want. What you really want. Tell me, and I'll do it for you."

I couldn't quantify my desire for this man. No unit of measure could rate this all-consuming feeling. But I had to retain some measure of control, or I would become totally lost in him. My fingers trembled as I undid Patrick's belt and pulled it from the loops.

"Could you put your hands behind your back?" I said in a hushed tone, shyly requesting dominance.

He did as I asked.

I looped the belt around his wrists to secure them. I unbuttoned his pants and coaxed down the zipper. His slacks slid down. I slipped off my clothes and tossed them aside. I lunged forward and kissed his taut chest, neck, and mouth. Skin-to-skin, I pressed closer, but it still wasn't close enough.

I slid Patrick's boxers down, and with featherlight kisses, I brushed my lips over him. His thighs flexed. He shifted as if trying to free his hands from behind his back. I looked up and met his gaze. Stormy and passionate.

I reclaimed his mouth and lifted a leg to hook it around him. My kisses remained hungry, and I positioned myself, ready to get as close as physically possible. And then I stopped.

"June? What is it?" he whispered.

A realization flooded through me. No matter what I did, I knew why I felt like I couldn't get close enough. By binding his hands, I had put up a blockade. To get closer, for true intimacy, there could be no restrictions, and no barriers.

The chemical reaction had to happen.

Patrick had shown me time and time again he was all in for me. He'd been patient. And tolerant with my "conditions." I couldn't ask for more. My heart swelled and busted down the wall. I was ready to let go of the past and move forward. To find love no matter the risk.

With my whole being, I trusted Patrick.

"June?"

I reached behind him and unwrapped the belt from his wrists. He stood untethered. Confusion crossed his face until he realized the choice I'd made.

He brushed my cheek with the back of his fingers and then followed with a tentative kiss. His hands moved gradually, haltingly, along my back as if waiting for me to put on the brakes. Not this time. My heart beat wildly, waiting for what would happen next. In a fluid motion,

Patrick swooped me up into his secure arms and carried me to bed.

Chapter Eleven

Weightless, I floated as Patrick laid me onto the downy duvet. I took in air and let it out. Breathing had never been this easy. My heart, mind, and body were absorbed in this magical moment. Patrick propped himself on an elbow. His skin glowed golden, the muscles of his chest and shoulders, highlighted and contoured.

He seemed uncertain and hesitant to make a move. By setting limits, I'd always been the one ultimately in control. Maybe he was cautious of taking the offensive position for the first time. Patrick and I were now equal players in the field. How would he express himself to me unrestrained? Anticipating his touch, goose bumps spread over my body.

"You take my breath away," he said in a low voice and smoothed some hair off my face.

My cheek tingled where he had touched me. The lines of his face were now so familiar. "You take mine," I said and reached behind his head to pull him closer. Our lips connected. The kiss explored and discovered. His fingers trailed a path along my neck and down to my chest. He swirled, teased, and cradled. Suspended pleasure registered through every microfiber.

Patrick's lips trailed down my abdomen, and then lower. Intense sensations overtook me, and I gasped.

He paused.

"Don't stop," I breathed, teetering.

He resumed contact and continued his oscillation. Coils inside tightened. I squeezed a handful of the duvet as I hit the pinnacle and was catapulted into a white burst. I floated in euphoria.

A dream.

Patrick moved over me; his hair scrunched in disarray.

I molded against him.

He needed no more incentive. Nerve receptors overloaded. Engulfed in a sensual haze, I was mindful only of Patrick. A tsunami wave gained momentum and force. A crested swell carried me, and I tensed as the wave crashed ashore. The powerful expulsion left me weakened and panting. Perspiration glistened on Patrick's body, and his chest rose and fell.

He moved to my side and held me close. My cheek to his chest, his heart thumped powerfully. Rhythmic, soothing. I closed my eyes.

Finally, content.

Finally, close enough.

When I awoke, I was still in Patrick's arms. I smiled lazily.

"I love you, June. It's the honest truth."

Had I heard right?

"I know it sounds crazy and rushed, but I've had feelings for you for a long time. Did you not sense it?"

"I thought you were persistent," I said.

He kissed my hand, and I knew I loved him, too. And I wanted to tell him.

The side of his mouth turned up. "So, you're not really a dominant?"

I shook my head. "No. Not at all."

"Not that I minded. You're hot as hell, no matter what you do."

"I don't understand what you see in me." I nuzzled in.

"I'm sure every guy sees what I see. Even Edward and Vinny."

I giggled. "Now you're being silly."

He lightly caressed my back with his fingertips. Relaxed and limp, I closed my eyes to feel his unhurried doting touch more completely. Was I lucky or blessed?

It was both.

I wanted to tell Patrick the real reason I needed to use the constraints. And now, because of him, I didn't need them anymore. To build on our relationship, I needed to be honest and tell him what my fear had been, even at the risk of him judging the reason for my kinky behavior.

"June?"

"Yes?"

"I hope you don't mind me saying this, but somebody must have done some number on you."

How did he know? Tears burned my eyes. He'd verbalized and validated my pain.

Something squeezed my throat, and it was difficult to find my voice. "I believed I had something rare with someone, and then he was gone."

He pulled me closer. I blinked, and a tear escaped from the edge of my eye.

Who would have thought I'd fall in love with the miserable cop I had at one time wanted to kick out of my house?

Chapter Twelve

Sheltered from a storm. A pea in a pod. A birdie in a nest. Half awake, I stretched as I thought of metaphors to describe how Patrick made me feel. Protected. Where I belong.

The smell of coffee wafted to the loft. I scrambled out of bed and pulled on one of Patrick's shirts. I smoothed my hand over my hair and tiptoed to the railing. Clad in only boxer shorts, Patrick was busy in the kitchen. I bit my bottom lip. Now that was a sight I could get used to.

He looked up. "Good morning."

I waved. "I'll be right down." I turned, and my phone alarm beeped in my purse on the floor. I grabbed it and noticed the water-damaged business card I had found at the crime scene. It completely slipped my mind to tell Patrick about it. I slid the card into the shirt pocket I was wearing.

Barefoot, I advanced downstairs. Patrick held a wood cutting board as a tray. On it sat a cup of coffee, a protein bar, a blue crocus flower in a shot glass, and a folded piece of paper tucked underneath.

He smiled. "My shirt never looked so good."

"I hope you don't mind."

"Mind?" He chuckled. "I thank you."

Flattered, I pressed my lips together in a smile.

"What do you got there?"

"Just a bite to hold you over until we grab breakfast somewhere."

"This is sweet of you, Patrick. Thank you." I reached for the folded note.

I'll never leave you, June.

P

Breath caught in my throat. His written words flowed like a protective, healing salve over my heart.

"Patrick—"

After our conversation last night, his note showed depth, understanding, and acknowledgement of the hurt I had gone through in my previous relationship. I took the board from him and set it on the counter. His bare chest had been inviting enough, but the man on the inside had become irresistible. I slid my arms around his neck.

"Where have you been all my life?"

He pulled me closer. "I can say the same."

He kissed me tenderly. And then it deepened. He cupped my behind and lifted. I wrapped my legs around his waist. He carried me effortlessly to the table. I clung to him as our bodies grew hotter. But then, disruptive thoughts intruded.

"I hate to say this," I said between kisses. "But do we have time?"

He paused. "Damn."

He helped me off the table and gave me a final kiss on my neck. Whew. I had to cool down. I sat on a chair and took a sip of coffee, fighting the urge to play hooky. I'd never played hooky before.

"I know we're pressed for time, but I'd like to show you something quickly," he said.

With curiosity, I waited and watched.

He put a black plastic briefcase onto the table and opened it.

"Oh, wow," I said. "Is this how a cop snags someone's heart?"

He chuckled. "Is it working?"

"I think so," I said, looking at three handguns on the gray foam insert.

"You don't have to choose now. Or I can acquire another model if you prefer something else." He handed me the first black one. It was heavier than it appeared.

"This Glock G19 is popular, easy to conceal, and is smaller than the G17. It has a 15-round magazine." He picked up the second black one. "This CZ P-01 is a perfect compact 9mm. Very reliable, and it also has a 15-round magazine."

His tech talk was impressive, but it sounded like he was speaking in another language. I picked up the Glock to examine it, and then the CZ. To my untrained eye, they appeared similar.

"When you hold a gun, babe, be sure to not to point it at anybody."

"Whoops, sorry," I said and aimed the weapon downward and put it back in the case.

I eyed the third one. I liked the look of the stainless-steel barrel.

"The last one is a Smith and Wesson 642. A compact revolver, but packs a punch."

My fingers curled comfortably around the black grip. The solid weight evoked a sense of respect and danger. "This one," I said.

"You don't want to think about it? Or shop around further?"

I shook my head.

"It's a high-quality gun. You made a good choice," Patrick said. He put it back in the gun case and locked it.

"Thank you, Patrick, for always watching out for me during these unnerving circumstances."

He drew me into an embrace. "You don't have to thank me, June." He kissed the top of my head, and his phone rang.

"Hello, Tom," he said.

I listened to the rumble of his chest as he talked.

"Do you have confirmation of that? I'll be in shortly." He hung up.

Reluctantly, I pulled away. "Duty calls."

His jaw tensed. "Yeah."

We readied ourselves and picked up a bite along the way. Patrick parked in the work parking lot, kissed me in the car, and then I trekked into the lab.

I said good morning to Lara and Edward sitting at microscopes and put on my lab coat.

"Is Vinny off?" I asked.

"No," Edward said. "He's giving our new recruit the tour."

"Oh, great," I said. Finally, some help was hired.

I headed to the refrigerator to get a glass flask of buffer solution. I turned and saw Vinny enter the lab with the new staff member. The shock of seeing the new hire drained the blood from my head and turned my legs into quivering gelatin.

"And this is June Harber," Vinny said to the man beside him. "June, I'd like to introduce you to Dr. Hamid, our new pathologist."

I gasped, and the flask I'd been holding smashed onto the floor.

Chapter Thirteen

Glass shards and buffer solution pooled on the floor around my feet. Without looking, I knew all eyes were on me, and lava heat burned my cheeks.

"Well, is everyone awake?" I added awkwardly to make light of my idiocy.

I heard chuckles, and Vinny bent down to help me collect chunks of glass.

"It happens to the best of us," Vinny said and turned to Dr. Hamid. "Despite this slip up, Doctor, rest assured that June is definitely one of the best."

"Thanks, Vin," I said and glanced up at the doctor.

He smiled, and my heart thumped like a jackhammer.

"I have complete faith in everyone here, especially June."

That deep voice with a rasp strummed familiar notes. I hadn't heard it in two years, only in remnants of memories. Was he really here? I needed to focus on my task. My hands shook as I threw a few pieces of glass into the sharps discard.

"Thanks, Vinny. I'll finish cleaning this up," I said.

Vinny groaned and dropped a piece of glass. His palm dripped blood. He cupped his other hand underneath and leapt to the sink.

Dr. Hamid strode over to Vinny. "You okay there?"

"Yeah, just caught a sharp edge," he said and held his hand under running water.

Lara retrieved the first aid kit and removed a bandage.

Disaster. I felt horrible. "Vinny, I'm so sorry you cut yourself."

"It's on me. I should have had the common sense to get a broom and dustpan, like Edward over there."

Edward was already sweeping up the fragments. From a cupboard I grabbed absorbent cloths and wiped the floor. I blew a strand of hair from my face, stood up, and tossed the soaked wipes beside the trash can. Of course, I'd missed and drew more unwanted attention. I grabbed the rags from the floor and shoved them into the bin.

Dr. Hamid watched, and I trembled inside.

Lara finished taping Vinny's hand and looked sideways at me. She missed nothing and had certainly noticed my agitation.

Dr. Hamid came over. "It's a lovely surprise to see you, June. Have you been employed here for long?"

"Two years. I've been here for two years now," I said, remembering all too clearly the circumstances that drove me to a job change. "I'm surprised to see you, Dr. Hamid. I thought you had moved out of state." I surprised myself, too, at hearing the assertion in my voice.

Beside us, Vinny flexed his hand with the new patch job. "Wait, you two know each other?"

"Yes," Dr. Hamid said. "We worked together at St. Eugene's for several years."

Edward Ying chuckled. "Small world."

Lara raised her brows.

"In that case, June," Vinny said. "Would you mind finishing the tour and showing Dr. Hamid where the morgue is? It'll give you a chance to catch up and discuss your case."

"Oh, sorry, Vinny, I actually can't take Aram, uh, Dr. Hamid, on a tour. I have to pH buffer for the next run."

"I'll do that for you," Edward said.

"No, it's okay. I can do it. Serves me right for dropping the flask. Right?"

But Edward had already grabbed a new flask. "No worries, June. Go ahead. Enjoy your reunion."

A groan escaped my throat. "Oh. Thanks," I said and turned toward Dr. Hamid. He grinned, and his cheeks dimpled in obvious amusement. Two years ago, he had macerated my heart, and now he acted like nothing had happened. How dare he?

"All right, Dr. Hamid, please come this way. I'll show you where the cooler and the autopsy suite are. Buckle up. We're so busy here you may never find your way out."

Chapter Fourteen

Aram and I walked down the barren hallway toward the steel elevators. This man had been my world. His breakup had devastated me, but also changed how I proceeded with my new cautious life, that is, until Patrick.

I had finally moved on from Aram. But right now, with him beside me, memories rushed back with his charming smile, the shape of his lithe physique, and the way he walked, smooth and assured like a jaguar. I tried to act calm and unruffled, but my heart beat erratically.

I pushed the elevator button and dared to take a glimpse when we got in. His bright aqua eyes still captivated.

"How are you, June?"

His voice. Deep and warm. I hadn't heard it in so long. It sounded like a replay of an old song. "I'm great, thanks," I said. "How have you been? How is your wife?"

Considering my blunt question, I expected an awkward silence. But there wasn't any.

Aram scrunched his brow as if he was carefully choosing his words. His words had always been wise. "I've been all right. I don't know if you had heard, but for the past two years, I've been in Scranton, working at the University Hospital."

"No, I hadn't heard where exactly you were. You didn't like it there?"

"I did. It was a very modern facility with all the latest technology."

"Then why did you come back?" The elevator landed at zero, and the doors opened. I didn't wait for an answer and got out. He followed me down the corridor, and I gestured to the right.

"This door leads to the locker room and showers. The number to the combination pad is 2-4-5-6. Do you want me to write it down for you?"

A corner of his mouth turned up. "No. I think I'll be able to remember it."

Of course, he'd be able to remember four numbers. I realized I was acting like a scorned shrew. This wasn't me. We continued to the next door, and I punched in the entry code.

"This is the main entrance to the morgue," I said in a softer, less formal tone as we entered a square tiled foyer. I pointed to the inner steel door. "Inside are the autopsy suites and the cooler drawers. We can house twenty-four bodies, and right now we are close to capacity. You're going to be busy," I added. My voice had trailed off. He made no move and had no hint of humor in his expression.

"I'm not afraid of a little work," he said.

My mouth went dry. Why did it feel like nothing had changed, when in fact everything had changed? His lips parted slightly. Our gazes locked for a few seconds. Or was it an eternity?

"Do you want to go in and look around?"

"I've missed you," he said in a low voice.

My breathing ceased. He missed me? There was a

time when I had yearned for him and hoped he missed me too, in some minuscule way. I filled my lungs and became lightheaded.

The door from the main corridor flew open, and Vinny stormed in, holding a folder.

"Oh, good, you're here," he said. "Enjoying the tour, Dr. Hamid?"

"Immensely."

I crossed my arms over my chest and fought for composure. "Since you're here, Vin, I'll let you take over. I have to head back upstairs."

"Wait, June," Vinny said and held up the file. "Did you fill Dr. Hamid in about the case you're involved in?"

"Um, no, I didn't," I said. "It's not really relevant."

"It sounds extremely relevant," Aram said. "Please, enlighten me."

"Okay." I swallowed. "Well, long story short, last week I happened to be in the wrong place at the wrong time and was assaulted in front of a house in which a body was found."

"Assaulted? How? Were you hurt?"

"I'm fine," I said.

Aram's eyes narrowed.

"No, really, I'm okay. I was just shoved to the ground."

Aram pressed his lips in a tight line. He looked worried, or angry, or both. Did he still care?

"June, tell him how you're connected to the victim in there," Vinny said and pointed to the cooler.

"Yes, please tell me," Aram said.

"After my spill I got up and noticed I had a few cuts, scratches, and Officer Verbeek took me to the hospital. As a precaution."

"He did the right thing," Aram said.

If Aram only knew. I tried to continue to focus on my explanation instead of him. "As it turned out, I had blood on my arm, but no injury. We figured out the blood wasn't mine."

"Then whose was it?"

"We're performing DNA analysis on it, but we're assuming it was the perp's blood, or the victim's," Vinny said. "And the perp's still on the loose."

"I don't like the sound of that," Aram said. "Are those documents from the case?"

"Yes." Vinny handed him the folder. "Mr. John Doe."

Aram flipped through the paperwork. "Are there any photos?"

"They're not in there?"

"No, none here."

"I'll have to check with the crime scene photographer about that."

"Thank you, Vinny. If possible, I'd like to get started on this autopsy today."

"That would help move the investigation along," I said, feeling more excited than I let on.

"June, I'd like to ask you more questions about this case. It'd be highly beneficial because I think there's more going on here than I know."

"Sure, but I don't know how much help I'll be." I backed up a step. "I really should return to the lab."

"Tell Dr. Hamid what he needs to know, June. It's all good. I'll keep covering for you." Vinny turned, and the steel door slammed behind him.

Aram and I were alone again. He rubbed the back of his neck. "June, I have a request, but feel free to refuse if it makes you uncomfortable."

I stiffened and didn't blink, afraid of the next words that would come out of his mouth.

"Would you be willing to assist me during the autopsy? Nothing heavy or too involved, just help with paperwork and collecting samples. And it would give us a chance to talk further about the case."

I signed in relief. Naturally, his request was work related. Even though his request pertained to the case, I wanted to say no.

"I don't have experience working down here, but sure, I'll try to help in any way I can."

"Wonderful. How about we meet back here in an hour?"

"Okay. One hour," I said.

I burst into the stairwell and cringed.

Sure, Aram, I'll help in any way I can?

Was today opposite day? I bound upstairs and went into an empty office beside the lab. If I was going to do this, I'd try to do it right.

I logged onto the computer and typed in "autopsy procedure." I clicked on the images tab. Row upon row, photos popped up of bodies in various stages of dissection. My stomach twisted, and I clicked out of the screen. I chose an article on procedural steps.

Autopsy, also called postmortem or necropsy, is the examination of a deceased body's anatomy and its organs...

The body is laid out on the examination table, appearance is noted...

Photographs and x-rays may be taken...

The pathologist makes a Y-shaped cut, from the shoulders, down the abdomen. Rib cage plate is removed. Organs are removed and sampled…

I clicked on images again. Never a fan of gore, these shots sickened my stomach. I logged off, seeing all I wanted to. I checked my watch and headed down to change into scrubs.

When I walked out of the ladies' locker room, Aram exited the men's at the same time. We both halted. Aram raised his brows and laughed.

"Fancy meeting you here," he said.

"Yes, what are the odds?"

His smile diminished, and he scanned the hallway in each direction. "June, earlier you had asked a question in the elevator, and I never answered."

I reached behind me to brace myself against the wall.

"Remember, you asked why I had returned from Scranton?"

I shrugged. "I was curious why you came back. It sounded like you enjoyed your new job."

"I did. It was an excellent facility."

Ever so slightly, he moved closer.

"But," he said in a quieter voice, "I thought it would be best to return here after my divorce."

Chapter Fifteen

Aram opened the door for me to the dark autopsy suite. I was still stunned at the news of his divorce. The smell of stale disinfectant steeped the air and reminded me of the imminent task at hand. He flicked on wall switches, and the ceiling exhaust fan roared. There was nothing inviting about the blue-white artificially lit room, gray nonslip floor, and stainless-steel autopsy table, sink, and shelves. Cool air chilled my arms, and I vigorously rubbed them.

Like in the photos, I imagined a body on the pedestal autopsy table, with a giant Y incision.

I swallowed a lump in my throat.

"June?" Aram said in a soft tone, frowning. "I'm sorry. I shouldn't have asked you to assist me, especially after what you've been through."

After all this time, Aram could still read me and sense how I felt. At one time, I had found these qualities more attractive and desirable than Aram's looks or status. But today, they were of no consequence because he had decided to leave me. I straightened my posture.

"I'm actually fine, Aram."

"Are you sure?"

"Positive. Now, shall we don our PPE? John Doe in the drawer over there isn't getting any fresher."

Aram chuckled. "No, definitely not. All right, let's

do it."

Let's do it. I snapped my mouth shut. Did he deliberately choose those words to make my mind wander? No, he wouldn't have. Or would he?

We pilfered the supply shelf along the wall, and each put on a long-sleeved waterproof gown, mask, face shield, and gloves.

"Would you know where the body diagram charts are?"

I rummaged through the wall file holder and found a set of sheets. "Right here."

"Perfect. Now let's get Mr. Doe." He wheeled a transport trolley to the cooler drawers. "Which number is he in, June?"

"Compartment five." I sounded more casual than I felt.

Aram swung open the door.

I gravitated closer. Coolness swirled around my ankles as I peered into the dark, lifeless recess.

Aram butted up the trolley to the open compartment and then yanked out the stuffed black bag. He wheeled the gurney over to the autopsy table. I plunged forward to help guide the body bag onto the examination table. Aram hit the foot pedal of the recorder. "Test, test."

"Ready to begin, June?"

I nodded.

Under my mask, trapped breath heated my face, and my heart pounded faster and harder for more oxygen. I swallowed to keep the gastric juices down. I became faint and panicked as my symptoms intensified.

Aram grabbed the zipper tab.

"Wait," I said and swayed.

"June!" Aram rushed over and put an arm around

my waist.

We retreated from the table. "Hey, how about we get you some fresh morgue air," Aram said and removed my face shield.

His voice soothed and lessened my distress.

I pulled off my mask. Air cooled my damp face, and breathing became a hundred times easier.

"That's better," I said.

"Got a bit woozy?"

"Yeah. This is embarrassing."

"You're not the first to get queasy. You should see all the first-year residents that go down."

He guided me to a chair and squatted beside me. "How about you go for a bite to eat? I can handle things here."

I couldn't disagree. "That'd be for the best. I'm sorry."

"Don't give it another thought."

There was a bang on the door, and Aram straightened up. "Come in."

The door cracked open, and Patrick stepped in. "Hello?"

"Patrick." I didn't know if I was more happy or more surprised to see him.

"Vinny told me you were down here. How are things going?"

"We were about to start the autopsy," I said and left out the details.

The men looked at each other, and I almost groaned at my predicament. "Uh, Dr. Hamid, this is Officer Verbeek. He's the officer that came upon the crime scene."

"It's good to meet you, Officer."

"Likewise," Patrick said. "Thank you for giving this case priority."

"Once I found out June was personally involved, I wouldn't have had it any other way."

"I appreciate that, Doctor. Taking care of our own," Patrick said.

Aram crooked a brow. "Yes, but there's more to it than that."

A noise escaped from my mouth. This scenario was getting a little too uncomfortable. I didn't want any personal issues to surface. There was no need to go there.

"Officer," I said quickly, to change the topic. "Dr. Hamid was just asking if there are pictures of the crime scene."

I could tell Patrick was suppressing a smile. I assumed he found my addressing him professionally amusing.

"Yes, there are several photos, but I don't have hard copies with me."

"Great," Aram said. "I'd like to see the shots. Vinny will probably contact your department about them."

"That won't be a problem. I can do you one better. The crime scene is still taped off. Would you like to visit the area yourself?"

Aram's eyes widened. "Yes, absolutely. That would be ideal. Is later this afternoon a possibility?"

I listened to the guys make a "date." Awkward didn't begin to describe this triangle.

Then they looked at me. Were they going to include me on their field trip?

"Count me in," I said. "I'm fully invested in this case, and you gentlemen are not going without me."

Besides, guys talked. I couldn't let my past

relationship with Aram come up in conversation. When the time was right, I wanted to tell Patrick myself.

Chapter Sixteen

After work, Patrick, Aram, and I bustled through the drizzling rain to the police cruiser. I grasped the back door handle.

"Have a seat up front, June," Aram said. "I always wanted to sit in the back of a squad car. It's my first time. Honest." Aram's chuckle was contagious, and we all laughed.

Aram leaned forward and spoke through the cage. "This ride will definitely be memorable."

"Hopefully not as memorable as the last time June and I headed to this address."

In the side mirror, I caught a glimpse of Aram's raised brows. "I'm wondering, why was June out patrolling with you?"

I bit my bottom lip. Aram's voice sounded casual, but I detected intense curiosity. I jumped in to answer his question. "I had missed my bus that day, and Patrick offered me a ride."

"I still regret putting her in harm's way." Patrick put a hand on mine.

I couldn't tell if Aram had noticed Patrick reach over. Normally, I reveled in his touch, but right now I couldn't enjoy it to its fullest extent because of the unwieldy situation.

"I'd like to clarify something," I said. "Patrick

hadn't placed me in any danger. What happened to me was, well, on me."

Patrick gently squeezed my hand before moving his back on the wheel.

"Still willful," Aram said.

Heat flooded my face. What possessed me to think it was a good idea to ride in a cruiser along with these two? This would be the first and last time. And definitely memorable for me.

Patrick parked in front of the taped-off house and turned off the ignition. He got out and opened my door first. Aram waited like a trapped detainee until Patrick released him.

"So, Doctor, how was the scenery from back here?"

"Excellent," Aram said.

"Don't get used to it," Patrick said.

"Haha." I laughed nervously.

"They have swabbed the area inside the house for DNA, and as far as PPE goes, I think only gloves will be necessary should we need to touch anything." He popped the trunk open, and we each grabbed a pair.

We advanced along the stone path. Leaves blew around my feet, and I noticed the hedge leaves turning shades of yellow. The hedge. I still had to tell Patrick about the business card I had found.

We skipped up the porch steps. Patrick removed the key from the lockbox and swung the door open.

"Who lives here, Officer?"

"Currently, no one. This is a vacant rental unit. Recently renovated."

We filed into the foyer. The temperature felt as cool as it was outside. I detected the smell of fresh paint. It was so quiet I could almost hear myself breathing.

Patrick flipped on the light. We walked on tiled flooring through a tidy galley kitchen. The quartz countertop was clutter free, and the porcelain undermount sink had no dirty dishes in it. There wasn't any evidence of any foul play here. And then I saw the wooden knife block with an empty slot.

We traipsed into the eating area. The table was askew, and chairs were knocked over—evidence of a struggle. A pool of brown-red blood crusted up on the floor, and there were streaks and spatters of blood on the floor, table, and wall.

"They're going to have to paint again," Aram said.

I held back a nervous giggle. He was still a jokester. "Is this where the victim was found?" I asked.

"Yes. He more than likely sustained his fatal injury here," Patrick said.

"From a knife wound?"

"That's what the good doctor will determine."

Aram intently scanned the room. "The knife wasn't the murder weapon."

"No?" I said in surprise.

"He was shot. The bullet nicked the iliac artery." Aram said. "My guess is there was an aggressor with a gun, and a victim, who grabbed a knife in self-defense."

"You're two-thirds right," Patrick said. "We suspect there was another person involved. We found three sets of footprints."

"Then probably two aggressors. What the hell went on in here?" Aram said, more to himself as he eyed every detail of the room.

"We've concluded one party had a key and entered through the front door. The second and third parties entered forcibly through the back door. And the altercation took place here, in the kitchen."

Aram bent down to look at the kick plate of the maple kitchen cabinet. "Is that a bullet?"

Patrick crouched. "That's exactly what it looks like. Forensics must have missed it."

My jaw dropped. "That's incredible."

Aram shrugged. "Just a lucky glance."

"I will have to get the team back here to extract it," Patrick said and took out his phone.

"Umm, Patrick." I moved closer to him, wishing I didn't have to ask what I had to ask at this particular moment. "May I use the bathroom?"

He put the phone back into his pocket. "Sure. It's this way."

"We'll be back in a minute, Doc. Look around and snap some pics."

"Will do," Aram said.

I followed Patrick down a carpeted hallway. He peered into each of the two bedrooms and then the bathroom. "All clear. You're good to go."

I snorted a laugh.

Unamused by his pun, Patrick shook his head. "I'll wait for you right here."

"Don't be silly. I'll be fine." I pursed my lips in an air kiss and shut the door.

"All right." He spoke loudly so I could hear him. "I'm going to make a call and check the basement."

"Okay!" I said as I placed tissue on the toilet seat, even though it looked like a clean bowl.

When I was done, I peeked out, left and right. I turned toward the basement stairs. "Patrick?"

I descended the steps. The basement light was on.

"Down here, June."

I stopped on the bottom stair. Debris from torn-down ceiling tiles covered the concrete floor. Areas of wood paneling had been broken in several areas. Along the back wall sat a dirty, ripped couch, which appeared to be more sliced than ripped.

"Looks like the renovations stopped here," I said. "This place is trashed."

"You noticed that, too?" Patrick said. "There may be asbestos down here. I prefer you don't come down without a breathing barrier. Go join the doctor. I'll be there in a moment."

I didn't move. I loved watching him in cop mode.

"Please go up, June," he said in a softer tone.

I turned to head back upstairs.

Aram appeared to be deep in thought as I approached him in the family room. He smiled when he noticed me.

"Feel better?" he said.

"Much," I said. "Find any more clues?"

"No. I'm just looking for more lodged bullets."

"It's amazing you found the one in the kitchen. You have eagle eyes."

"I do my best," he said.

Seemingly out of nowhere, a question popped into my head.

"Aram, I was wondering about something."

"What's that?" His eyes brightened.

"Would you by any chance know a Dr. Fulthorpe?"

"I know a Stan Fulthorpe."

"Really?"

"They awarded us our fellowships the same year. But he received his in hematology, if this is the Dr. Fulthorpe you're referring to."

"I believe it is." My heart played hopscotch.

"Why do you ask?"

"I came across his name." I didn't want to explain about finding the business card until I spoke with Patrick.

"Stan works at St. Eugene's, and I know he has a long wait list of patients. Excellent doctor. And a true gentleman. Not a rogue like me," Aram said with a slight smile.

I coughed and glanced behind me to see if Patrick was in earshot.

"It's none of my business, June, but are you and the officer seeing each other?"

He had seen Patrick's hand on mine in the car.

I nodded. "Yes. We are."

"Lucky man," Aram said. His eyes glistened.

Approaching footsteps startled me to silence.

"How is it going?" Patrick said.

Aram's gaze lingered on me for a second longer. "I think I've seen all I need from here," he said. "Thank you for the excursion, Officer."

I too was ready to be gone from this place and the dynamics of the situation. There were too many emotions and secrets at play. And I couldn't shake the dark suppressive energy of the crime scene.

I noticed the snap was open in Patrick's holster. He had been ready to protect. And then I noticed him holding a plastic ziplock bag with something white in it. "What do you have?"

Patrick lifted the bag. "This is a piece of ceiling tile I found on the basement floor. It has a stain."

I took the bag from Patrick and then showed Aram.

"If I were a gambling man, and I am," Aram said, "I'd wager that is blood."

Chapter Seventeen

Patrick parked in the Police and Forensic Complex lot.

"Thank you for the outing, Officer," Aram said, as we traipsed up the concrete stairs to the building's entrance.

"You're welcome. But it's me who has to thank you for finding that slug," Patrick said.

"I'm glad I happened to be looking down," Aram said and scanned his badge. The door unlocked with a click.

I always liked Aram's humility. If anyone had reason to boast, it was him, but he didn't. He downplayed his intelligence and achievements.

"Thanks again, Officer," Aram said. "June, I guess I will see you tomorrow?"

"Yes, Dr. Hamid. Have a great evening."

Aram continued down the hall to his office.

"Can we put this piece of ceiling tile into evidence and be on our way?" Patrick said.

"Of course." We walked to the lab, and I flicked on the lights. As I expected, everyone was already gone for the day. I put my purse on the bench.

"How are you doing?" Patrick asked. "You're quiet."

"Am I?"

"Did being at the crime area upset you in any way?"

It had. I twisted my shoulder forward in a half shrug. "How do you do it, day in and day out?"

"It's a job. I've become somewhat desensitized. But once in a while, something will throw me."

He got a faraway look. Perhaps one day I'd question him about this more, but not now. I wouldn't push the conversation anymore. I moved forward and kissed him lightly on the lips and slipped the zipped bag out of his hand. I sat in front of a computer and entered the ceiling tile into evidence.

Patrick chuckled. "Smooth move. Before long, we'll have you working undercover with the force."

"God help the force," I said and remembered my sleuthing the week before. "Actually, I have something to tell you." I bit my bottom lip.

He came over and sat on a stool beside me. "Yeah? What's up?"

"Do you remember the night of the storm last week?"

"I do. I had to work late that night."

"Right. Well, that evening I went for a drive to the crime scene."

"On Landry?"

I nodded.

He furrowed his brows. "Why? You didn't go inside, did you?"

"No, no. But I walked around the house. And I asked a neighbor walking her dog some questions."

His face slackened into a smile. "Like I said. You'd be an asset."

"I really don't know why I went there. I guess I was hoping to face fears. And maybe recall more details."

I walked to the steel refrigerator and placed the bag inside with the other evidentiary items.

"Did you remember anything?" he asked.

"No. I just roamed about the yard. It was getting dark, and it poured. On the dash to my car, I saw a speck of white under the hedge. I dug it out and discovered it was a business card. I've been meaning to show it to you, but I figured it was probably nothing. But then I thought it may be something."

"Do you have it with you?"

"No, it's at your place."

"What was on it?"

"On the front, it had the name of Dr. Stanley Fulthorpe, Hematologist. And on the back, in blue ink, is the Landry address."

"One-o-nine Landry?"

"Yes," I said. "Maybe it's a clue. Right?"

"It very well could be. You've had this card for how many days, and you're only telling me now?"

"I've been meaning to show it to you. At first, I didn't think it could be related to the case."

"June, next time, if there's a next time, please tell me what you find as soon as possible. No matter how insignificant you think it may be. Deal?"

He was right.

"I'm sorry. I should have. I just—." I sniffed and fought tears in a wave of oversensitivity that was probably hormonal. Patrick wrapped an arm around me.

"Hey, don't apologize," he said quietly. "You did great finding that card, June. I'll pay a visit to Dr. Fulthorpe in the morning."

I breathed in his subtle bergamot aftershave. I closed my eyes and leaned into him.

"June?"

"Yes?"

"Why don't you come with me tomorrow to see Dr. Fulthorpe? Before you start work? It'd be an asset having you there to help me with medical lingo."

"I'd love to go. And I'm sure Dr. Fulthorpe will be very helpful. Aram says he is a kind, very well-respected man."

"Aram Hamid?" he said.

"Yes. I asked him if he knew Dr. Fulthorpe."

Patrick rubbed his brow with his fingers. "You told Dr. Hamid about who was on the business card before mentioning it to me?"

"Yes, but it's not like that. Aram and I were just talking at the crime scene while you were in the basement."

"Right," Patrick said. "But which is it, June? Aram or Dr. Hamid? How well do you know this guy, anyway?"

"Pretty well. We used to work together." I bit my inner cheek. Omitting the truth was the same as a lie, and that meant I had just lied. I would tell Patrick the truth about Aram and me. But not tonight.

The opening door startled me. Charlie, the security guard, walked in, sporting a newly cropped brush cut.

"Hello, Officer. June. How are things?" He adjusted the two-way speaker on the left upper area of his safety vest.

A tad awkward, I thought. "We're just getting ready to leave for the night."

"Well, I won't keep you two. Just doing my rounds. Have a good night, folks," Charlie said and walked back out.

Patrick looked at me. "Ready to go?"

"Am I ever." I stood and adjusted my top.

The side of Patrick's mouth curled as he looked at the top button of my blouse. It was possible we were going to skip dinner and go straight to dessert. I was more than fine with that. And I was glad we dodged any further conversations about Aram's and my past.

For now, anyway.

Chapter Eighteen

Patrick and I grabbed takeout burgers and fries for dinner on the way home. Once inside the kitchen, I put the paper food bags onto the table, and Patrick set down the drink tray. He removed his gun and utility belt and deposited them into a cabinet drawer.

"I'm just going to get out of these clothes," he said.

That was an attractive picture. I beamed ear to ear.

He chuckled. "I'll be right back."

I took two plates from the cupboard and pulled the drinks from the cardboard tray. I snatched a French fry from a bag. This day had been completely opposite to my old usual routine. From morgue to crime scene, pin balling, so to speak, between two men. I had no experience in crime investigation, but I felt I wanted, no needed, to dive into all this more. I couldn't figure out why, because I hadn't particularly enjoyed the day's occurrences.

Patrick came back wearing sweatpants and a T-shirt. He sat and took a sip of his fountain drink. "Nickel, for your thoughts?"

"For you, no charge," I said. "But seriously, I was just thinking about the day."

We put the burgers and fries on our plates and dug in.

"How are you coping?"

"I think as good as can be expected. But—"

"But what?"

"It's hard to explain. I feel that this is all, anticlimactic. We have gotten no answers. Just more questions."

"Welcome to investigative work, love. It's not like what you see on television."

"Not at all. Right now, I am so happy with you, but with regard to the case, it's like I have a black emptiness inside. I can't describe it."

Patrick looked at me in thought. "Black emptiness? Like a void of missing something? Or someone?"

I froze. What was he referring to? This couldn't be about Aram. Could it? Was I being paranoid? Had my imagination gone wild because I hadn't yet told Patrick about Aram and our past?

"I don't feel like I'm missing anything," I said.

"June, I think I know what you're going through."

"Really?" I said as I crinkled up the foil wrappings from our meal. Internally, I braced for the truth of our conversation.

"The dark emptiness you feel right now. I've experienced it before."

"You have?"

"Yes. I believe you're involved in this case deeper than you realize. Personally, professionally. And we can't dismiss how you may be in danger."

He had a valid point. Since the day Patrick answered that police call while driving me home, my life had changed. I had become consumed by unanswered questions, tension, and fear. If Patrick wasn't beside me, I'd certainly be living in terror.

"I've never been inundated like this before," I said.

"You can only live on adrenaline for so long, and then you crash," Patrick said. "Tomorrow, perhaps you shouldn't come with me to visit that hematologist, Dr. Fulthorpe. Maybe it'd be best to slip back into your usual routine."

"Perhaps, but I want to go tomorrow. I need to."

He gave me a sympathetic smile. "It's addictive, isn't it? Needing answers. Craving justice."

His gaze pulled me in, as did his insightful words. I did need answers. And I'd always wanted fairness and justice for everyone. I remember even at an early age sticking up for kids that were teased at school.

"Yes, this really is all-consuming. How were you able to figure out what I'm going through?"

"All I've figured out is I've felt the same way you just described," he said. "I also suspect you're longing to make passionate love to me right now."

I laughed. "You couldn't be further off the mark, Officer."

He jumped out of his chair, scooped me up, and slung me over his shoulder. Like a caveman, he carried me upstairs, and I giggled. He set me on my feet beside the bed, and I wrapped my arms around his neck.

"What would I do without you?" I whispered.

He frowned. "Without me, you wouldn't be in this mess."

I caressed his neck. "That's not true. I got myself into this mess, remember?"

"Well, we won't harp on this anymore." He put his lips to mine and pulled me close. Our kiss lingered and deepened, heating me inside and out. We undid each other's shirt buttons and laughed at the awkwardness of our tangled arms. He sat on the bed, and I stood between his thighs. His expert mouth moved across my cleavage. He was in no hurry to unhook my bra. I closed my eyes, relishing the sensation. My hands cradled his neck, and then I ran my fingers through his hair. I floated as if without gravity.

Behind my closed lids flashed an image of Aram. Dark hair, brows, lashes, electric aquamarine eyes. Breath caught in my throat, and I stepped back, winded.

Patrick looked up at me, as if he was just wrenched from a dream. "Hey," he said softly. "You okay?"

"More than okay." I moved to continue where we had left off. He undid the button on my pants. They slipped down, and I stepped out of them. "Stand up for a sec," I said. He obliged, and I undid his trousers.

He kissed my shoulders and slipped his arms around my body. Before he could unsnap my bra, I angled away from him.

Shit.

What was wrong with me?

His lips parted as if about to speak, but he remained silent. I had behaved in this manner when we had first become intimate. And now I was re-enacting that same push-pull.

Aram. It was because of seeing Aram I'd regressed into this mode. I didn't know what else to call it.

"June," Patrick said. "It's all right. How about we just cash out? We have an early morning planned." He stood and pulled back the bed sheets.

"Stop," I said. I would not let phantom emotions from the past impede on being with Patrick. I'd do what I had to do to get past it.

He stopped and crooked a brow.

"Stay there. Don't move," I said and dashed out of

the room. I leaned against a wall in the hallway to catch my breath. Breathe, I told myself. Breathe. Wait. I had an idea.

I scurried down the stairs to the wall unit. I turned on the stereo and found a station with melodic pop music. Perfect for upping an intimate atmosphere. In the kitchen, I opened the top drawer of the cabinet and retrieved what I wanted. I raced back upstairs and paused in the doorway, short-winded from running. Panting wasn't overly sexy, and I hoped he wouldn't notice.

Shirtless, Patrick's triceps flexed as he pulled down the window blind. He turned, and his mouth curved into an affectionate grin. "You put on music."

"I did." I pushed my shoulders back and jutted out a hip. I took my hand from behind my back and held up his handcuffs. "Once more, for old times' sake?"

His eyes scanned the entire length of me. I'm sure he soaked in every detail. He was, after all, a cop.

"You're taking me on what charge?" he said.

"For being the sexiest man I've ever known."

"In that case, I surrender."

Chapter Nineteen

Light kisses on my shoulder roused me from sleep.

"Hmm, good morning," I said in a low voice.

"Good morning, my goddess of the hunt," Patrick said, his soft breath at my neck.

I smiled. Yes, he could say that. I had, after all, captured and contained him with his own handcuffs. My eyes sprang open. "Patrick, your hands. Are they okay?"

He opened a hand, made a fist, and opened it again. "All good. Circulation is back."

I cringed at the thought of having locked the cuffs too tight. "I feel awful. Why didn't you say something?"

"I, uh, didn't want to interrupt," he said.

I brushed his cheek. "You are being too nice. You should've charged me with assault." I traced his lips with my finger, and he gently took the tip between his teeth. I smiled and inched closer until bare skin touched bare skin. Heat transferred, and energy pulsed between us.

Patrick glanced at the handcuffs on the night table.

"No. We don't need those," I said.

"Sure?"

I nodded.

In a swift motion, he pulled the covers away and rolled to hover over me. His kisses devoured hungrily, even after last night. How could that be? Never mind. I would not question it, just go with it.

From the night table, the tinny sound of Patrick's phone alarm sounded. He appeared not to hear it, but then pulled away to look at his phone.

"I hadn't realized the time." He sighed. "We should get ready."

"If we must," I said and kissed him on the nose. We shifted and got on our feet. I went over to my travel bag and rummaged through limited clothing choices.

"Want to jump in the shower first?" he said.

"No, go ahead. I have to sort things here," I said.

"I won't be long," he said and disappeared into the hallway.

Today's outfit would be a soft pink tunic and paisley printed jeans. I placed the items on the chair in the room's corner and started making the bed. My phone beeped with a text message from an unfamiliar number. I clicked on it, and my heart leapt.

—*Good morning, June. This is Aram. I hope you don't mind, but I asked Vinny for your number. He said you'd be in later, but I want to make sure you're okay. Maybe yesterday was too much for you.*—

I read the message again. No, this wasn't cool.

Patrick entered the bedroom wearing a towel around his waist. I logged out from the text screen and tossed the phone on the bed.

"I put out a fresh bath sheet and facecloth for you." He opened his closet. "Hear from anyone?"

"What? No, just checking my emails. I'll go shower now."

Once in the bathroom, I shut the door and collected my thoughts. Aram's unexpected text startled me. But what I found most disturbing was my reaction to it. I'd lied. My heart pounded. My past relationship with Aram loomed over me like a dark heavy cloud.

I squeezed toothpaste onto my toothbrush. There was a firm knock on the door, and I jumped like a jittery squirrel.

"June, want eggs and toast?"

"Sounds wonderful," I said.

Absently, I looked at my reflection in the mirror, thinking of my situation. I had hesitated too long. It was time to clear the air. Patrick would probably never feel the same way about me again. And he may never trust me again. But before we went any farther in our relationship, he had to know the truth. I had had an affair with a married man. He had been separated at the time, but I should have stayed away, nonetheless. And that man had been Aram.

The timing would never be right, but I couldn't bear to keep this secret about my spotty character any longer. I wouldn't leave this house until I told Patrick what I had done. I was ready for his reaction, which would probably be in the range from disappointment to breakup.

I joined him in the kitchen as he took orange juice from the fridge. I eased myself onto a chair at the table.

"Thank you for breakfast," I said, but I didn't reach for my fork.

"No problem. Juice?"

"Sure," I said, and he poured me a glass. I took a sip.

Patrick hadn't started eating yet. He looked at me as if he was assessing a motor vehicle accident, and I was the mangled metal. I shifted in my chair. Seconds felt long, and awkwardness hung in the air. He sensed my solemn mood.

I nibbled on a wedge of toast, mentally preparing for my confession. "Patrick, I need to tell you about a past relationship."

"No, June. You don't need to tell me anything."

"But I think it'd be best to get skeletons out of the closet now, before we get involved any further. Don't you agree?"

"Maybe. Maybe not. I'm usually non-reactionary, but if you tell me this person harmed you, I'd have to hurt him."

His willingness to come to my aid without question soothed my heart. "I wasn't hurt, physically. But in that relationship, I was to blame as well. I had behaved badly. I—"

"June, how about we leave it all in the past?" he said. "Is it all in the past?"

I nodded. "Yes. Completely."

Tightness released from my chest, and his kindness filled my heart. I picked up my fork.

As we ate, Patrick opened his black notepad. "I'd like to quickly review our next steps with Dr. Fulthorpe, if you don't mind shop talk for a minute."

"Not at all," I said lightly.

"Perfect," he said. "I called the hematology clinic and found out Dr. Fulthorpe starts seeing patients at eight in the morning, so we'll arrive before that time. We'll begin by presenting him with the court order, which arrived via email sometime last night." He glanced at me with a subtle smirk, most certainly caused by thoughts of us being too preoccupied the previous evening to check our emails.

He sobered his expression and continued speaking. "We'll play it by ear. Ask questions and see how far we get. This may be a short meeting. He may not have a clue as to why his business card was found in that location."

I nodded and crossed my arms over my chest.

"Perhaps when introducing yourself you can mention you're a lab scientist and you are working with forensic pathologist, Dr. Hamid on this case. Then we can see how he reacts. Gauge how forthright he is about divulging personal information about being acquainted with Dr. Hamid."

I wasn't comfortable setting this doctor up to evaluate his reaction. But Patrick had his operating procedures and certainly knew what he was doing. "I'll give it a go," I said, trying to sound upbeat.

"Great. It's a plan," he said and finished his drink. "Try not to be nervous, babe. This could be a lead, and it's all because of you."

His empathy touched my heart. I cared for him. Loved him. So very much.

Suddenly, I had a fear of losing him.

Chapter Twenty

Patrick and I arrived a few minutes early at the hematology clinic at St. Eugene's hospital. A blonde ponytailed receptionist arranged files on her desk.

"May I help you?" she said and batted her fake eyelashes at Patrick in police uniform.

"Ms. Harber and I would like to speak with Dr. Fulthorpe," Patrick said in a clear, firm voice.

"He should be in soon," she said. "You're welcome to wait for him."

"Thank you," Patrick said. The waiting room was empty, and we sat in the chairs closest to the entrance.

I shifted on the hard, cold plastic seat. The magazines on the table beside us were in disarray, so I straightened them into a neat pile. I kept glancing down the hallway we had emerged from.

"Are you all right?"

"Yeah. I just don't know what to expect, I guess."

"Neither do I," he said with a wink.

And just like that, in three words, he brought a smile to my face.

"Before I forget, I want to tell you I have to work late tonight. I'll give you my house key," he said.

"You don't have to. I can stay at my place."

"I'd prefer you didn't."

"You still don't think it's safe?"

"I don't."

"I actually need to pack a few more things. And I have to check for mail and water my plants."

He shook his head.

"I promise I'll be fast. I'll go right after work when it's still light out."

One of his brows rose in a doubting expression, prompting me to convince him further.

"You can weaponize me. Lend me your baton, or stun gun."

He thought for a second. "Pepper spray. I'll give you a cylinder to use until I give you a shooting lesson."

"Deal."

"And check your front and back doors. Do not go in if they've been opened or tampered with. I'll duck out and meet you there, if I can."

"Check front and back doors. Gotcha, Officer." Were these security measures all part of his job, or was he being overly protective of his woman? I hoped it was the latter, because if not, I was in more danger than I realized. Like a bad meal, that thought didn't sit well with me.

About ten minutes had passed when patients started checking in and occupying seats around us.

"I wonder how much longer the doc will be," Patrick said and looked at his watch.

"Maybe he's delayed with rounds or something."

"Possible," Patrick said.

A man in a toque walked past us, sat a few chairs over, and unzipped his jacket. He peered at Patrick. The others in the waiting room stole glances as well.

I leaned closer to Patrick. "I think you're drawing attention."

"The uniform does that," he whispered.

"Nah. I don't think it's the uniform."

His mouth curved into the slightest smile, and he checked his wristwatch again.

"Should we have Dr. Fulthorpe paged?" I asked.

"That's a good idea."

Patrick had barely finished speaking when a man in a cream linen suit, matching hat, and shoulder bag walked briskly into the room and went to the front counter. He spoke with the receptionist and then turned to look at us.

"That might be him," I said.

"Let's find out," Patrick said. We both stood and trekked to the reception desk. "Dr. Fulthorpe?"

"No, Dr. Gideon Crawford."

The doctor's heavy spicey cologne made my nose tingle.

"Do you know when Dr. Fulthorpe will be in?" Patrick said.

"It doesn't look like he'll be in today. Can I help you with anything?"

"Ms. Harber and I wanted to speak with him for a few minutes. Do you know why he won't be in?"

"I'm assuming he needs time off."

"Do you work with Dr. Fulthorpe?" Patrick pressed on.

"Yes. We're co-owners of this center."

"Can you call us if he shows up?" Patrick handed Dr. Crawford a business card.

Dr. Crawford glanced at the people sitting in the waiting area and lowered his speaking tone. "Would you like to tell me what this is about, Officer?"

"We are inquiring about a person of interest. We'll

keep trying to contact Dr. Fulthorpe. Thank you for your time."

"Very well, Officer, Ms. Harber."

Dr. Crawford walked away, and I sprang forward to catch up with him. "Dr. Crawford, do you, by any chance, have a business card? In case we need to contact you?"

He stopped. "Of course," he said and pulled a card from the side pocket of his bag. "I'll write my cell number as well." He took a shiny gold pen from his shirt pocket, scribbled numbers on the back, and then handed it to me.

"Thank you very much."

Dr. Crawford moved his lips into a smile that looked forced.

"One more question, Doctor, if you don't mind," Patrick said.

"I don't mind, but patients are waiting. What would you like to know?"

"Has Dr. Fulthorpe ever not showed up for a clinic?"

Dr. Crawford's eyes darted. "Not that I recall."

"Thank you for your time. We won't keep you," Patrick said.

"Good luck with your case," the physician said and scanned his badge to unlock the door to his office.

Patrick and I headed out of the waiting area and strolled down the corridor.

"Where the heck is Dr. Fulthorpe?" I said.

"Good question. I'll try to contact him this afternoon. What did you think of Crawford?"

"He seemed very curious about what we were there for. And his cologne almost knocked me over," I said. "So much for the scent-free policy. I guess rules don't apply to doctors."

Patrick chuckled as he opened the door. We stepped outside into the early sunlight and headed to his squad car. He drove me to work and walked me to the lab.

"Will you be okay finding your own way to your duplex?"

"I'll be fine."

"Be careful. Scout out your property and apartment." He opened a snap on his belt and removed a narrow cylindrical can. "Here, take this with you."

"Pepper spray? I thought you were kidding." I took it from him and slid it into my purse.

His concern warmed the intangible part of my heart. With him, I didn't sense any danger, which perhaps wasn't a good thing. But it showed how much I trusted him.

He kissed me on the cheek.

"Have a good day," I said.

"It'll be a long one without you," he said softly.

I smiled at him before I entered the lab but sobered when I saw all the new sample bags piled on the bench top. Vinny sat at a computer with his back to me, Edward pipetted solution into rows of gel wells, and Lara was speaking to someone on the phone. The room hummed with the sounds of the overhead exhaust, the high-capacity centrifuges, and the DNA sequencing machines. No one seemed to notice me until Lara turned and hung up the phone.

"Hi, June," she said as I buttoned up my lab coat. "It's great to see you."

"You, too. What do you want me to do first?"

"Good morning, June," Edward said.

Vinny looked back and waved.

"Hi, guys," I said.

Lara shut off the centrifuge. "June, if you don't mind, you can add fluorescent label to that run."

"Sure," I said and retrieved the reagent bottles from the refrigerator.

Vinny stood from his computer and came over. "Good news, June. The DNA results from your case will be ready today. They're on the analyzer now."

"That is great," I said. "Thanks for rushing them." My stomach fluttered. The sooner they found the killer, the better and safer for everyone.

"No problem," Edward said as he came over and reached for some papers on the counter. "A perk of the job. Besides, working with a dream team."

Lara snickered and rolled her eyes. "June, did you hear we've hired another lab tech? Our so-called dream team is increasing by one."

"That's fantastic," I said.

"Yeah," Lara said. "And you may know her. She used to work at St. Eugene's."

I dropped onto a stool beside me. They had hired someone I used to work with?

Oh, God, please don't let it be Victoria.

Chapter Twenty-One

In the lunchroom I sat at the round veneer table, alone with my thoughts and an oat bar. I was relieved to hear my ex-colleague Victoria hadn't been hired to work here in forensics, but Ursula, another "difficult" ex-workmate, was. In this moment, it didn't matter. I had more important things to worry about, and I tossed the half-eaten bar into the trash and headed back to the lab.

The DNA results from my case were almost ready. I paced the aisle. Would we finally have the name of a potential murderer?

Lara looked over the top rims of her glasses. "How much longer?"

"Twenty-two minutes." I tapped my fingers on my crossed arm. "Oh, twenty-one," I said when the number changed on the screen.

Vinny wiped the counter with a disinfectant cloth. "Soon, June. Hopefully, the suspect is in the police database."

"I'll cross my fingers," I said. "But what if he's not? Then what?"

"Then the police keep investigating," Lara said.

Of course, they would. But it'd be so much easier if the police had a name.

Vinny cleared his throat. "Would you two mind if I head out a bit early?" He raised his brows and reminded me of a sheepish schoolboy asking a teacher for permission to go to the bathroom.

"Fine with me," I said, as I watched the instrument timer count down another minute.

"Sure, Vin," Lara said. "Hot date?"

"Kinda," he said. "It's my fifth wedding anniversary. I've gotta pick up a card."

"Nothing like waiting 'til the last minute," Lara added and pushed her glasses to the bridge of her nose.

"Lots of time," he said.

I laughed. "Not really, Vinny. How about you pick up some roses, too? One for every blissful year."

"Chocolate is always appreciated. So is a gift card," Lara said.

"Five years is a milestone, Vin. I think you should write her a poem professing your undying love," I added.

"Or your undying horniness," Edward said as he walked by.

Lara and I cackled in laughter.

Vinny rolled his eyes. "You people are hysterical."

"Give us a full report tomorrow," Lara called out to Vinny as he walked out the door.

The analyzer hummed, only minutes away from completing its cycle. Hopefully soon, by the genius of modern technology, we'd catch a criminal.

"Where did Edward go?" I said.

"He has a meeting with Dr. Hamid. Computer software issues, I think."

"Oh." A powerful beat thumped deep in my chest. Shit. I willed my body to stop reacting to the mere mention of Aram's name. I reached into my pocket and took out my cell phone.

—Hey, Patrick,

Hope you're having a good day.

The results we've been waiting for are minutes away.

XO—

The sequencer machine made a grinding sound, and a high-pitched tone sliced the air. An alarm icon flashed on the screen, but I didn't know why. Lara sprang from her stool and came over. She pushed a button to silence the alarm, and then scrolled to the error log.

"It says pump disabled and run aborted."

"What? How can that be?" I swung open the front door of the machine and checked the sample trays, the electrodes at the back, the pump, and polymer bottle. I made sure no tubing had become detached. "Everything seems okay," I said and closed the lid. This was unbelievable. It's like I had jinxed the analyzer by staring at it too hard. "Now what?"

The door to the lab opened, and Edward Ying entered. He reached behind the instrument and turned off the power switch.

"Wait. The results," I said, but too late.

"We have to reboot. There are middleware issues affecting all departments, but I fixed it. I just got Dr. Hamid's computer up and running. The results should be saved on the instrument's hard drive," Edward said.

The three of us watched the screen light up again and run through start-up checks. Finally, the home screen appeared. I held my breath as Edward brought up the day's work list.

Empty.

The list was empty.

"Hmm," Edward said and shrugged. "Must have been a glitch."

"A glitch? Are the results gone?" Lara asked.

My insides sank.

"They probably are. We will have to repeat the tests on an overnight run," Edward said. With a few taps on the screen, he started the reanalysis of the samples still in the instrument. All wasn't lost, just delayed.

"Well, shall we call it a day?" Lara said.

I looked at the clock on the wall. "Yes, let's call it." I draped my lab coat on a wall hook and took my bags from the back desk.

"Do you need a ride, June?" Lara asked.

"Thanks, but I can catch the five o'clock bus."

"Sure?"

"Yes. But thanks anyway. I appreciate it."

We walked out of the lab into the hallway when I noticed Dr. Hamid heading in our direction.

"Hello, ladies," he said. He smiled at me in a special way.

"June, if you have time, I'd like to ask you a quick question about the autopsy."

My heart raced. He spoke professionally, but I sensed this had nothing to do with work. "Sure, Dr. Hamid," I said. "But can this wait until tomorrow? Lara offered to drive me home."

He didn't hesitate in responding. "Yes, absolutely. Have a lovely evening, ladies," he said and retreated down the hallway.

Lara glanced over her shoulder at me as we stepped outside.

"Do you mind me taking you up on your offer after my blatant refusal?" I asked.

"Of course not." We weaved through the parking lot, and Lara pushed a remote to unlock the doors to her car. "I'm hoping one day you'll tell me what just happened in there."

"I'll fill you in. I promise."

Lara smiled. She knew I was being coy, but she didn't question me further along the ride. She pulled up in front of my apartment.

"Thanks so much for the lift, Lara. See you tomorrow."

"No worries," she said.

I got out and waved as she drove off.

As I had promised Patrick, I visited my duplex apartment in the light of day. I checked the mailbox and removed flyers and a bill. I unlocked the front door and latched it behind me. Inside, everything seemed in order, but nonetheless, I was wary and ready with my pepper spray. I wished I hadn't come here without Patrick. Uneasiness twisted my insides, knowing a stranger had been in the downstairs of my apartment. My personal, private living space. I'd do what I came to do and leave before it got dark.

From the kitchen tap, I filled a plastic watering can and drenched my snake plants at the side window. I hustled into the bedroom, chose a few outfits, and put them into a plastic bag. At sonic speed, I finished doing what I needed to do and called for a cab.

"ABC Taxi, hold please."

I scrolled through the phone and saw Patrick had received and opened my message but hadn't responded yet. I hoped everything was okay. And then I thought about the basement. I had the urge to go downstairs and take a peek—make sure everything was secure.

I jumped when the woman started speaking again.

"We'll have a car there for you in about twenty

minutes," the taxi operator said.

"Okay, thank you," I said and hung up. Twenty minutes?

My fingertip rested on the pepper spray button as I opened the back door and headed down the stairs with half trepidation and half curiosity. I found the key under the mat and unlocked the door. Daylight streamed in. Eerie quietness filled my ears, but all seemed fine. I glanced around the cluttered basement and almost walked face first into a web hanging from the ceiling. I squealed and backed away and shook with the heebie-jeebies.

I grabbed a broom and brushed away the cobweb. From an askew ceiling tile, something silver dangled and reflected light. My curiosity got the best of me. I dragged an old kitchen chair over and climbed onto it. Upon having a closer look, the silver item was a ball bead chain. Like a keychain. I reached for it and took it down but found no keys. Instead, there was a black rectangular object, smaller than a lighter. And then I realized what I had found.

The oddest thing to be located in the ceiling.

Chapter Twenty-Two

In the back seat of the taxi, I examined the USB stick I'd found in one hand and held my mobile phone to my ear with the other. This was my third attempt at calling Patrick. Why wasn't he answering? My stomach tensed, and I tried to tell myself not to fret. But I worried anyway. The driver slammed on the brakes at a red light, and I palmed the seat in front of me.

My phone vibrated, and I swiped to answer. "Hello."

"June, how are you? Are you at my place yet?"

"I'm on my way now."

"Great. I'm finishing up here."

"Was work busy?" I asked.

"I wrote reports for most of the day."

If he had been at a desk, why hadn't he answered my calls? "Oh, really? Because I tried calling you a few of times, but they went to voicemail."

I heard myself speaking and didn't like how mistrusting and skeptical I sounded, even to my own ears.

"Sorry about that. Is everything all right?"

"Yeah. I just wanted to fill you in on what happened in the lab today. But I can tell you about it tonight." The taxi turned down his road. "I'm almost at your place."

"You have my house key, right?"

"I do."

"I won't be too much longer, babe."

"Can't wait to see you."

"Me too."

I hung up, and in a short while, the cab pulled into Patrick's driveway. I plucked bills from my wallet and paid the driver. Inside the house, I dropped my bags at the door, flipped on the lights, and proceeded into the kitchen. I opened cupboards and came upon a package of pasta and a jar of sauce. In the fridge, I found ingredients to make prima vera.

I washed veggies in the sink and looked out the window at the expansive yard. The setting sun approached the barn and forest tree line. Rays reached like outstretched arms in a bright finale. I watched in awe. But then I noticed shadows forming. Soon, the darkness would offer easy refuge to anyone out there who sought it.

I yanked on a cord and shut the slatted blind.

The days were getting shorter, grayer, and gloomier. Patrick's farm home, while warm and comfy, felt barren without him. I couldn't describe my current mood, except that my emotions fluctuated between being scared, uncertain, and paranoid.

I chopped the peppers, zucchini, and an onion. The bulb's fumes burned my eyes, and I retreated from the invisible vapors. I wiped tears with a tissue, retrieved my bag from the front hallway, and carried it up to the bedroom.

I placed my clothes in a drawer Patrick had emptied for me, and I hung a blouse and a pair of pants in the closet. My phone beeped with a text.

—On my way.—

I breathed easier, knowing he'd be here soon.

On the floor, my purse gaped open, and I reached for the flash drive. I sat on the bed and turned it over in my hand. What could be on it? Documents? Photos? Porno videos? I tried to figure out what I should do with it. Even though I was curious as to why this USB resided on a ceiling tile; I should have left it where I found it. I'd put it back into the basement and perhaps mention it to the landlord. But then I noticed Patrick's laptop on the side table.

No.

The content of the drive wasn't any of my business. I turned and headed downstairs to the kitchen. Hopefully Patrick had a hankering for Italian.

I continued preparing food. There was a large pot in the cupboard under the sink, and seasonings in a drawer. I moved the spice bottles until I found the oregano. And then I noticed an empty pill vial—narcotic pain medication prescribed for Patrick. The floor creaked beside me, and I dropped the bottle and slammed the drawer.

"Oh, hi," I said to Patrick as my heart pitter-pattered.

From behind, he slipped his arms around my waist. "What's cooking?"

"Pasta, veggies, and sauce, is that okay?"

"More than okay," he said and kissed my cheek. He backed away and poured himself a glass of milk. "So how did your place look? No signs of unlawful entry?"

"Everything appeared secure. Is that how you say it?"

Patrick chuckled. "Yes, it is. Are there any results from the case yet? I didn't check in."

I stopped stirring the sauce. "I called to update you."

"What's the update?" he said.

Was he intentionally avoiding accounting for my missed calls? I couldn't let this go.

Boiling water overflowed and sizzled on the stove.

Patrick jogged over, slid the pot off the element, and turned the knob.

I grabbed a tea towel, wiped up the excess water, and wrung the cloth over the sink.

"I appreciate you making dinner."

"And for making a mess?"

"There's no mess." Patrick slid his arms around me again. "I'm sorry I didn't return your call. What did you want to tell me?"

"I wanted to give you an update."

"Has the case finished sequencing?"

"Not yet. There was a computer glitch, but the repeat run should be ready first thing in the morning." I grabbed Patrick's hand. "Come," I said and pulled him behind me. "I want to show you something in the bedroom."

"Lead the way, darlin'."

I laughed as we headed up the stairs. I sat on the bed, took the flash drive from my purse, and held it up.

"I thought you were going to show me something else, but I'll play. It looks like a USB stick."

I nodded and waited for him to ask more questions.

"What's on it?" he said.

"I don't know. It's not mine."

"Whose is it?"

I shrugged. "I have no idea."

He scratched his nose and smirked. "Where did you get it?"

"I found it at my place," I said. "Downstairs."

"In the basement?"

"Yes. Above a ceiling tile. At a crossbeam."

Patrick walked around his bed to get his laptop. "Let's have a look," he said and booted up his computer.

I handed him the drive. "You think we should?"

"Who will know if we do or don't?" he said and inserted the stick.

And just like that, he solved my moral dilemma of whether I should look to see what was on the drive. I leaned closer when he clicked open a file.

A list of names appeared, each with accompanying twelve-digit numbers.

"What do you think that is?" I asked.

"I don't know. My guess would be this is a business listing of some sort. Clients, maybe with invoice numbers. Or maybe passwords."

"How many are there?"

He scrolled down, page after page. "A hundred, maybe two," he said. "I can't find a business name, address, or logo anywhere." He scrolled to the end of the list. "That's all we got. A list of names and numbers." He removed the drive and handed it to me.

"Thanks," I said in an underwhelmed voice.

"Not what you were expecting to find?"

"I didn't know what to expect. At least it didn't contain any sleazy videos."

"Well, that could easily be added. We'll just pop that back into the computer port and hit record." He swooped in and kissed my lips and neck. "But to do that, these clothes have to go."

I giggled as he pulled my top over my head.

Chapter Twenty-Three

I startled awake and checked my cell phone on the night table. The alarm wasn't set to go off for another half an hour. I turned to see if Patrick was still sleeping. He wasn't. He was on his back with an arm above his head.

"You're awake, too?" I said.

"Yeah. Bad dream, babe?"

"I think so. Can't remember. It looks like you're contemplating something."

"I am."

"What?"

"I'm thinking about the pending DNA results. And The Espresso Bar and Eatery."

"Oh, yum. Is that where you bought those breakfast sandwiches before?"

"Yes."

"Well, the run comes off the analyzer in about an hour. Think we can make it to the Eatery before work?"

A smile curled on his lips, and a devilish glint flashed in his eyes.

As if a track official had shot a gun to start a race, Patrick and I kicked off the sheets and scrambled out of bed. We moved around each other, getting showered and dressed, adding a kiss here, or a loving touch there.

Along the way, we drove to the takeout window for

his coffee and sausage breakfast sandwich, and my tea and a morning glory muffin.

"Yum," I said as I took a bite of the warm muffin top, wishing I had ordered two of them.

Patrick slipped his hand to my knee.

In what seemed like no time, we were at the police complex and parked near the lab entrance. We carried our beverages, and I scanned my new ID badge to get into the building.

The first to arrive in the lab, I flicked on the lights and headed straight to the genetic analyzer. Patrick trotted close behind. I tapped the instrument's screen to initialize the warmup. We took sips from our cups while waiting in anticipation.

"You know, Patrick, I have never eaten or drank in the lab before," I said. "This is a serious safety violation."

"I don't want to be in violation," he said.

"There's no one here," I whispered. "I won't tell anyone if you won't." I couldn't believe I just said that.

"Sounds covert," he said. "I've never seen this secretive rebellious June before. Tantalizing."

The lab door swung open.

"Oh, good morning, June, Officer," Edward said. "Results ready yet?"

Patrick discreetly took the cup from my hand and tossed our drinks in the trash.

My mouth twitched into a momentary smile.

Smooth move, hun.

"Hi, Edward," I said. "The results are loading right now." I tapped on the screen and selected the specimens of interest from my case. My heart thumped. The first DNA test report appeared on the screen. I read the allele numbers. Patrick moved closer to the display. Edward came over too.

"Unfortunately, the John Doe in the morgue will remain a John Doe. His DNA is not in the database," I said. "And there weren't any identifications from the crime scene either."

"They may be illegal entrants," Patrick said. "What about the blood I swabbed from your arm?"

I scrolled to the next field. "There were two sets of DNA found."

"Any identifications?" Patrick asked.

"A male and a female," I said.

"Any matches from the convicted offender's index?" Edward asked as he inched closer.

"No matches. But the one thing this confirms is the blood wiped from my arm probably belonged to the perp, not the dead victim. I'm assuming the female DNA is mine, from skin cells wiped off my arm—a contaminant, so to speak. I'll confirm that, to be sure." I had hoped for a suspect identification, and in an instant my hope was obliterated. I fought pangs of disappointment. We still didn't know who the victim was, or who the guy was that knocked me flying.

"Well, that stinks, Officer," Edward said and moved to another computer.

Patrick rubbed his neck. "It does. It would have been preferable to have a name."

My phone rang, and I grabbed it from my pocket. Private caller. "Hello?" I heard some sort of rustling. "Hello?"

The connection was cut off.

Patrick's eyes narrowed.

"Wrong number, I guess," I said.

"Did they say anything?" Patrick asked.

"Not a word."

"What's the number?"

"It was private." I shrugged. "Probably spam."

Patrick paused and seemed to be assessing what I had said.

"I'm going to head out, June. I'll pick you up at five?" he said.

I pursed my lips for a quick air kiss. Patrick opened the door just as Dr. Hamid entered.

"Thank you, Officer," Dr. Hamid said as Patrick held the door open.

My knees weakened, destabilized. Damn visceral reaction. Aram smiled at me. Oh, those dimples.

"Good morning," Dr. Hamid said. "Is there any conclusive news?"

I shook my head. "There's no match."

His lips pressed together. "Not ideal."

Edward pivoted his eyes sideways at us as he walked by.

"I won't keep you, June," Aram whispered. "I'd like to have a quick chat about the other day. But it can wait."

"I have time now," I said and tried to figure out what Aram could have been referring to. He gestured with a head tilt, and I followed him into the hallway. "What's up?"

The clip-clopping of shoes echoed in the corridor, and Aram paused from talking.

Lara Armstrong approached. "Was there a fire alarm?"

"No alarm," I said. "Dr. Hamid and I are just talking about a case."

"That's a relief. I was afraid the autoclaves

overheated again. Good morning, by the way," Lara said.

"Good morning," Aram and I harmonized.

I waited until the lab door closed. "Aram, you've got me curious."

"Sorry, I'm not trying to be cryptic. I wanted to let you know I had an odd occurrence, or coincidence, happen."

"Really?" He had me stumped. I had no clue where this could be going.

"Remember asking me about Dr. Stan Fulthorpe?"

I listened intently. "Yes, I do. At the house I had inquired about him because his name was on a business card I had found on the property."

"Perhaps it wasn't so random."

"How?" My mouth dropped open.

"I have privileges, and I do consultations at St. Eugene's. Yesterday I attended hematology rounds at the hospital," Aram continued.

He licked his bottom lip before speaking. He had full lips. I backed away from him slightly.

"Stan Fulthorpe's partner, Gideon Crawford, had presented a talk on bone marrow transplants and antirejection medications."

Patrick and I had spoken with Dr. Crawford at the hospital. "I've met him," I said. "He seems—"

"Seems what?"

"Odd. Don't you think?"

Aram chuckled. "You're putting it nicely. He's an ass. A very wealthy ass. And a prominent member of all the exclusive clubs."

"I'm not surprised," I said. He was, after all, a doctor, and a specialist.

"No, I mean obscenely wealthy," Aram emphasized.

"For example, I buy art prints. But he buys originals."

"Oh," I said and tried to comprehend having that kind of money.

"Anyway, while presenting, Crawford spoke about a patient case of his office partner, who is of course, Stan Fulthorpe."

"Ok?" I said, trying to follow this thread.

"You're wondering where I'm going with this?"

I nodded.

"Gideon Crawford had mentioned that his partner, Dr. Stan Fulthorpe, wasn't present at grand rounds because he had taken an unexpected trip. And Gideon also said, in jest, that maybe Stan had been the mysterious winner of the Mega Moola Lottery and was in the Galapagos Islands."

"An unexpected trip?" I parroted.

"I don't think a destination is significant at this point," Aram said. "I'm mentioning this because I found it odd how you had asked about an old classmate whom I haven't thought of in years, and then I hear about him MIA the very next day. I assumed you would want to know."

"I do. And thank you. I will let Patrick know; he may want to question you further. Is that okay?"

At the mention of Patrick's name, Aram's chin tilted downward.

"Yes, of course, June. I'll do anything to help find the person who hurt the only woman I've loved."

I froze.

He looked down and rubbed his forehead. "I'm sorry. I shouldn't have said that. But you know me. I always say what I feel. I hope I haven't made things too awkward between us."

"Aram—" I didn't know what to say as his aqua eyes pulled me in.

The lab door opened, and Lara peeked out. "June, can I load the next run?"

"Ah, yes, I'll be right there," I said to Lara. I walked to the door and turned back to Aram. "Can we talk more later?"

"I'd like that," he said.

I never thought I'd ever see him look at me in that desirous way again. For two agonizing years, I had longed for him to come back. But he didn't. He had left me, and I had moved on. I walked through the lab with the most expressionless face I could muster up.

No, Aram, you've fooled me once, and never will again.

Chapter Twenty-Four

From beneath the glass fume hood door, I reached in and examined the piece of ceiling tile Patrick had submitted for evidence. The steady hum of the negative pressure exhaust deafened my ears to other sounds in the room. I scraped off the reddish-brown areas with a scalpel and immersed the bits into a tube of extraction fluid. It was odd to have had ceiling tile come into play in my life in two different ways. First in an investigation, and second, at my place in the basement.

"June!"

I jumped and swiveled on my stool to look behind me.

"Sorry, I didn't mean to startle you," Vinny said and pushed up his glasses. "Your previous co-worker, Ursula, is starting today. After she puts on a lab coat, I thought she could shadow you for the day."

"Oh, right," I said, recalling last week's announcement. My stomach twisted into a Palomar knot. I couldn't lie. She'd burned me before, and now I was twice shy.

Ursula entered the lab and walked toward Vinny and me. She hadn't changed. She still sported an edgy burgundy bob, winged black eyeliner, and wore a form-fitting lab coat.

"Hello, June," she said in a smooth voice and spoke

as if we were long-lost friends.

"Hi, Ursula. Welcome to forensics," I said.

Vinny placed a stool beside me. "I'll leave you two ladies to catch up. You're in expert hands, Ursula."

"I know I am, Vinny," Ursula said smoothly. "I'm the one who trained June, once upon a time."

I struggled not to grimace. I equated that training to boot camp. A long day stretched ahead. I took a deep breath and explained the extraction procedure. "As you can see, forensics differs completely from routine pathology."

Ursula didn't agree or disagree.

"There are SOPs online so you can familiarize yourself with what we do here. Have you been given a password yet?"

"I have," she said.

"That's good," I said. Moments of awkwardness were almost palpable, but I fought through them and kept talking about work duties. "For obvious reasons, it's especially important at this stage of sample prep not to cross-contaminate."

Ursula nodded, as if she knew everything already. That was good. At least she was engaging.

"Do you know if Aram is in today?" she asked out of nowhere.

"He is," I said as I screwed on the test tube lid, trying not to sound surprised or annoyed.

"I'll have to stop by his office and say hi," she said. "We had such good times together at St. Eugene's."

"I'm sure he'd like that," I said and pulled off my gloves, wondering how good those times really were.

"You know, June, things went to shit after you left St. Eugene's."

I paused. "Really? How?"

"We were understaffed, and everyone became stressed and bitchy. And of course, Victoria kept making mistakes, right up to her suspension. Thank God, you reported her. She would have killed someone."

"Thank you," I said, assuming that was a compliment. "Still, it was a tough thing to do."

"I'm sure it sucked, being labelled as a snitch," she said.

I bit my lip.

"Victoria was pissed," Ursula continued. "I'd never seen her face as red as when she came out of the boss's office. I'm glad to be out of that place."

"Me, too," I said. Finally, we were in an agreement about something. In her own way, I sensed Ursula was being respectful and cooperative. But only time would tell.

I showed Ursula the various instruments and briefly explained their function. We sat at a computer terminal, and I orientated her on the software program.

Ursula checked the clock on the wall.

I hadn't realized it was almost noon. "You're welcome to go for lunch. We can meet back here in an hour."

She got up and bustled out of the lab. The upside to training her was I didn't have to tell her things twice.

I remained seated at the computer and checked my work emails. I leaned back in my chair and thought of the mystery list on the USB I had found. I stood to retrieve it from my locker.

Halfway down the hallway, Ursula and Aram stood near each other. They were all smiles and giggles, and I said, excuse me as I walked by.

I rushed into the locker room and let out a breath. Their brazen flirting irked me. Maybe it was because Aram had seemed to have moved on so easily. It didn't matter now. That part of my life was over. Gone. I wasn't feeling any form of jealousy right now. I opened my locker.

What was wrong with me? Aram and Ursula were probably just catching up because they hadn't seen each other in a long while. I rummaged through my handbag and retrieved the USB stick.

The main door opened, and Aram sauntered over. "How are you?"

"Awesome."

He looked at my hand. "What's that?"

"Just a USB drive."

"Are they photos? Any of us?" He raised his brows and smiled.

I slammed the locker door. "No. There are no photos."

"I'm sorry, June," he said. "I saw the way you looked when you walked by, and I just wanted to say I am not interested in Ursula. Nor was I ever interested in her. I know it's moot now, but I wanted you to know."

My temper flare dissolved. He had read my expression of disgust and addressed unspoken words, unspoken emotions. His consolation smoothed my unjustified, immature outburst. "It's okay," I said.

"I'll see you around," he said and turned to leave.

"Aram," I said. "This stick actually isn't mine. I found it in my basement."

"Found it? Do you know what's on it?"

"A long list of names. And numbers."

"Phone numbers?"

"No. There are too many digits," I said. And then I couldn't believe the next words out of my mouth. "Actually, could you have a quick look? Maybe you'll know what kind of list or directory it could be."

"Sure. We can use my office computer, if that works."

"It does."

We made our way inside his office and left the door open. I handed him the flash drive, and he inserted it in into his laptop. He clicked the mouse until the list came up.

I shuffled closer. "I don't recognize any of the names, but of course I never expected to. There are no logos, subtitles, or dates."

He scrunched his brows in thought. "No, I don't recognize any names either. This looks like a personal compilation." He put a finger to the screen and counted the number of digits beside the names. "Twelve," he said. "A phone number has ten."

"Right," I agreed.

"Wait a minute," he said. "There are twelve digits. I don't know if this is a coincidence, but patient identification numbers have twelve digits."

Chapter Twenty-Five

At the end of my shift, I cleaned the bench tops with disinfectant wipes and snapped off my gloves. "Good night, everyone," I said to the group.

"See you tomorrow," Lara said. The telephone rang, and she answered it. "Forensics. Please hold. June, it's for you."

I turned. Who could that be?

"Hello," I said. Dead air. "Hello? Patrick?" I heard muffled sounds, and then the call ended with a click.

Lara had been watching.

"Faulty connection, I guess. Did the caller sound like Patrick?"

Lara shook her head. "I don't think so. It was a man, though. Quiet voice."

The phone rang again, and I snatched the receiver. "Forensics."

"Hey, June," Patrick said.

"Did you call a second ago?"

"No."

"Oh."

"Why?"

"Someone just called and asked for me. And then hung up."

"A second hang up today?"

"It appears so."

"Okay. I'm going to put a trace on those calls," Patrick said. "June, could you come to my office? I'm not quite wrapped up for the day."

"They'll let me in?"

"Bring your badge, and you'll be fine. I'm located close to the front desk."

"Okay," I said. "See you soon. I hope."

I advanced down the corridor, connecting the police station to the forensic building. In the reception area, a uniformed male and a female officer sat behind a long counter.

I held up my identification. "I'm here to see Officer Verbeek."

The female officer, sporting a tight bun, pointed to the hallway. "Go ahead."

I continued until I found the right door number.

I peeked into the plain office. Patrick sat on a black padded chair at a desk besieged with folders. "You know, you really should try to get an office with a window. And maybe a plant."

He gave me a weary smile. "I will put in a request. Please, have a seat. Can I get you anything?"

I sank onto a sturdy wooden chair. "I'm good."

He shuffled folders, put them aside, and clicked the computer mouse. "June, I traced the prank call you received this morning."

"Already?" I said more to myself.

"Yes. I know people." He winked. "That first call originated from St. Eugene's hospital. But the tracing stops there. We're unable to determine the extension from within."

"That doesn't really tell us anything. Does it?"

"Not really. I'm having the second call traced as we

speak, and we'll see if that search yields anything. On another note, I want to update you on the victim we found in the house."

"You've identified him?"

"He's still a John Doe."

"What? He had no identification? No fingerprint matches? Or tooth records?"

"No none." The side of Patrick's mouth turned up. "You're sounding more and more like a detective, babe. And you are irresistible. But I got to focus here."

Butterflies flapped in my stomach.

"This guy, more than likely, came here illegally."

"So why was he murdered?"

"Good question. My best guess is that it was an all-out brawl over something," Patrick said. "The interesting find is the murdered man wasn't the renter, or owner of the property."

"Then whose house is it?"

"It belongs to Dr. Stanley Fulthorpe."

"Wait," I said. "The hematologist who disappeared? Whose card I found?"

"The one and the same," Patrick said.

"Whoa. What could all this mean?" I thought hard about these pieces of information. Did they even belong to the same puzzle? "Is it a coincidence Dr. Fulthorpe disappears after a body is found in his house?" I asked.

"I would say it's no coincidence," he said. "But we need a motive. I think the key is with the guy who assaulted you. I checked with all the neighboring houses and none of them had any video surveillance that could help the case."

"Feels like a dead end."

"We have to keep digging. And we must remain

vigilant."

I nodded. "Right."

The telephone rang. "Officer Verbeek." He grabbed a pen and wrote on a pad of paper. "Thank you." He put down the phone. "We have a trace on the call you received in the lab, at 4:48 p.m. It originated from Jackson Variety Store—2449 Jackson Road."

My eyes widened. "Just across the street?"

"Are you up for a quick jaunt?"

"Absolutely." My heart pounded.

"Are you sure you're comfortable coming?"

"With you? Always!"

Chapter Twenty-Six

Patrick and I burst out of the front doors of the police station. The wind blew a chill, and I turned up my jacket collar. We waited for cars to pass before we crossed the road and headed to the strip mall. Patrick's eyes never stopped scanning the sidewalk, parking lot, and I took a cue from him. I hustled along at his side and searched for anything out of the ordinary, a familiar face, or a sudden movement.

The shopping center had a dozen or so businesses including a computer repair shop, Dairy Delish Ice Cream, a diner, and, on the very end, Jackson Variety—the convenience store, where someone had dialed my number.

Patrick held the door open, and we entered the shop. A man with a receding hairline slid a pack of cigarettes into his lumberjack shirt pocket on his way out. The tall wiry clerk with a wet mop haircut stood behind the counter and watched us as we approached.

"Can I help you?" he said. "Coffee? I can make some fresh."

"No, thank you. I'm Officer Verbeek, and this is Ms. Harber. We work across the street. My colleague here received a call from this phone number at 4:48 p.m., and we're trying to acquire the caller's identity. Was it you who had made that call?"

"No, not me. I just started work at five," he said.

"Could you give me the contact information of the employee working earlier? I'd like to speak with him, or her."

"That would be, Shaan. He's a dude, and I believe he is still here in the back. I'll go check."

"We'd appreciate that," Patrick said, and the clerk trotted off.

I looked at Patrick and raised my eyebrows. "Colleague?"

He stifled a smile.

A slim guy wearing a jersey and baggy pants approached.

"Are you Shaan?"

"Yeah."

"Hi, Shaan, how are you?"

The youth plunged his hands into his pockets. "I'm good."

"Good to hear. Shaan, we'd like to know if you made a call from the store landline at 4:48 p.m. today?"

"No, I didn't," the young man said.

"I have documentation of a call originating from this store's landline," Patrick said with inarguable authority.

"Y-yes, there was a call made, but not by me. Some guy came in here, emptied the change from his wallet, and bought an energy drink, before asking to use the phone. I dialed for him, to make sure it wasn't long distance."

"Did you know this person?" Patrick asked.

"No, never seen him before."

"Can you describe him?"

"Yeah, he was taller than me. Short, dark brown hair. Maybe in his thirties."

"Did he say anything?" I asked.

"He said his cell battery was dead, and he had to call his girlfriend at work."

I froze. A chill stroked my spine.

"Are there any other details you can remember about this customer?"

Shaan shook his head. "No. Except maybe he was white, like pale white. He was kinda hunched. Didn't look well."

"In what way?" I said.

"He looked sick. Maybe he was on drugs or something."

Patrick readied his notepad and pen. "Shaan, would you mind giving me your contact information in case we need to ask further questions?"

"Sure," he said and supplied Patrick with details.

We stepped outside, and I turned to Patrick. "Was I supposed to be the 'girlfriend' he was referring to?"

"I'd say that is a fair assumption."

"I have a stalker?"

"Not if I can help it."

Patrick stayed close to me as we crossed the road and got into the cruiser. During the drive to his place, I noticed Patrick glanced in the rearview mirror more than usual.

"Do you think we're being followed?"

"No," he said and gave my hand a reassuring squeeze.

When we arrived at his home, he escorted me in and bolted the door afterward. He peered out of the front window, unbuckled his utility belt, and dropped it onto an end table. He came over and pulled me into his arms for a full-on kiss. All engulfing, passionate, mind-numbing. He slowly pulled away and led me to the couch. He could have led me anywhere, and I would have followed. We sat, and he put his arm around me.

"Before I get completely unruly, we need to talk."

"I'm amenable to that," I said.

The side of his mouth lifted. "Amenable to the talk, or me getting unruly?"

I laughed.

His expression turned serious. "With regard to our case, I believe we've stumbled on something we've yet to figure out, and from here on in, we're going to have to be more cautious."

"Okay. But more cautious, how?"

"Go nowhere alone. Don't go back to your apartment. Your address is visible on public listings. If someone wants to find you, you'll be a sitting duck. And finally, *always* carry your weapon."

"Weapon?"

"Yes, the one you chose, and the one I'm going to show you how to shoot." He reached beside the sofa and picked up a black plastic case the size of a lunch box. He dialed a combination and opened it. Inside sat the revolver I had chosen. The seriousness of this case climbed tenfold. The most frightening part of this mystery was the uncertainty of how it would end.

"Want to try a few rounds before it gets dark?"

"Okay," I said, although there was no "okay" about any of this.

He picked up the revolver. "As you know, guns always have to be treated like they're loaded."

He cocked it to check it and looked down the barrel.

"The barrel's clear. Here on the side is the safety switch. And of course, you know where the trigger is.

Never hold the gun with your finger on the trigger. That's how accidents happen."

He handed me the cold, heavy weapon, which felt surreal in my hand. I practiced loading the bullets. Patrick guided my hands to show me the proper technique. He handled the weapon expertly, smoothly, professionally. After familiarizing myself with the firearm, we went to the rear of the property. About five yards away, there was a poster of a human silhouette on a wooden board.

Patrick released the safety. Arms straight ahead, he pointed at the target, anchored his shooting hand with the other one, and pulled the trigger. Bam. He shot the figure in the head.

"Wow, you're good," I said.

He chuckled.

My turn. I stood with my feet shoulder width apart. Patrick helped position my arms as I aimed. I steadied my hands as much as I could and fired. The gun's kickback surprised me, and more surprisingly, I had hit the target's shoulder. Adrenaline surged through my veins.

"Great shot," Patrick said. "You've disabled your target. Try again."

I fired six more rounds and emptied the cylinder. I lowered the gun and pointed it at the ground. My arms shook from the "workout."

"You hit the target with every shot, and the final round struck a kill zone. You're a natural, June."

"Nah. I'm just standing close to the human target thing."

"You did good, babe."

"Thanks, but—" I struggled to articulate my fear and

trepidation. The gun in my hand wouldn't allow me to minimize the seriousness of the situation any longer. I'd just traded in my pepper spray for a lethal weapon. Even if I was in danger, would I be able to bring myself to shoot someone?

"How about we wrap it up for the day?"

"Sounds good," I said with immense relief. I ensured the cylinder and barrel were empty and handed it back to Patrick.

Patrick repeated the safety check. "I want you to carry that at all times," he said.

His intense eyes scared me.

Was this case more dire than I thought?

Or was there something he knew he wasn't telling me?

Chapter Twenty-Seven

The chime of Patrick's cell phone startled me from a sound sleep. He answered it before the second ring, and I fumbled around for my phone to see what time it was. Eleven thirty p.m.

"Hello," he said. "Matt. What's happening?"

I stayed still as Patrick listened.

"When? Right now?" Patrick said. "I'll check it out."

"Who's Matt?" I said, widening my eyes to see in the dark.

"He's a buddy from the station, calling to give a heads-up."

"This late? That doesn't sound good."

"It's not. The house on Landry is on fire."

"The crime scene?" I uttered, stunned. "Is it arson?"

"I'd say that's a definite possibility." He turned on the night table lamp.

"We're involved in something big, aren't we?"

"We'll have to find out exactly what that is," he said and stood to get dressed. "I'm going to check out the scene. I'll be back as soon as I can."

"Oh no you don't." I jumped out of bed. "I'm coming, too!"

****

The flashing lights of the fire trucks and police cars

served as disorientating beacons of disaster. I tried to avert my eyes from the strobes of light that were making me nauseated. Or maybe it was the stress of the situation. Patrick and I parked on the fringe of all the activity and got out of the car. Smoke and acrid stenches thickened the night air. Part of the roof had collapsed, and the firefighters continued to drench the house even though flames weren't visible.

I forced a swallow.

"Are you okay?" Patrick asked.

"Yeah, I'm just not used to being so close to something like this."

"How about we go for a walk? Want to check the periphery? Sometimes arsonists like to watch their handiwork," Patrick said.

"So sick," I said. We walked up the street, checking to see if any person was sitting in a parked car, or if anyone was hiding behind bushes or shrubs. I pulled out my phone and hit the video record button as we paced the area.

Patrick smiled. "Very resourceful."

"For an amateur." The neighboring houses stood in darkness. There was no movement in or around cars, foliage, or trees, but I kept recording anyway. A few neighbors in pajamas stood on their front lawn, watching the commotion. A hunched woman held a hand to her face.

After a walk up and down the street, we returned to Patrick's vehicle.

"I saw nothing out of the ordinary, did you?" Patrick said.

I shook my head. "No."

"How is your recording?"

I hit play on my phone. "It's dark. And pixilated."

Patrick leaned over my shoulder and watched. "Nothing is really discernible."

"I should have turned on the torchlight. Oh, well." I slipped the phone into my handbag.

"Video surveillance was a great idea, June. Now, how about we try to have a word with the captain?"

We advanced toward the bustling scene and found a firefighter beside a rumbling firetruck. He clutched a two-way radio close to his mouth. "Is the house negative for occupancy?"

"Yes, negative, Chief," a crackled voice said. "The fire is controlled. We're just wetting down hot spots."

"Great news, Meyer. We'll initiate salvage operations in the morning." The captain turned toward us.

"Hello, Captain?" Patrick said.

"Wes Butler," the man said.

"May we have a word?"

"Yeah. You are?"

"This is June Harber, and I'm Officer Verbeek. We're investigating a crime that was committed in this residence."

The captain nodded. "They made me aware there had been a murder inside."

"Chief, do you have any indicators as to the cause of the blaze?"

"This fire had high intensity. It burned hot and fast. We won't be able to make assessments until tomorrow."

"My guess is arson for crime concealment," Patrick said.

"Mine, too. But vandalism, pyromania, insurance fraud, or even an act of revenge have to be considered as well."

Firefighters clomped by in their heavy boots, rolling up hoses.

"I'll stop by in the morning," Patrick said.

The captain nodded. "The team will still be here. And the fire marshal, if you have any further questions."

"Thank you," I said to the chief. "And be careful."

Patrick and I headed back into his car. He smiled. "Be careful?"

I shrugged.

He put his arm around me. "You couldn't get any sweeter if you tried."

"Neither could you."

Along the drive home, my mind raced as I tried to imagine how and why the fire had started. Maybe the murder suspect who was still on the loose doused the place with gasoline. I shivered.

"Are you tired?"

I shook my head. "Not really. You?"

"Would you mind if we stopped for a pizza?"

"I could go for that," I said.

Patrick ordered from a pub, and we picked up the pizza on the way home. At the kitchen table, he opened the box. The smell of fresh bread and pepperoni made my mouth water.

I grabbed a slice and bit off the triangle tip. I was hungrier than I thought. "This is great."

"Eat up," he said and took a slice for himself.

I paused before taking another bite. "Is it just me, or does it feel like this case is becoming more obscure?"

He nodded. "It's not just you."

"What is your plan or your next move?"

"There are several areas to look into."

"So many things have happened. Where do you start?"

"Here." He finished his slice and then ripped off the top of the cardboard box and pulled a pen out of his shirt pocket. "Let's get a visual." In the center, he drew a house and then added items as he spoke.

"There are several unconnected events—the house with a body, a suspect running away, your assault, your house break-in, the business card you found, the two phone calls, and the house fire. The most dominant areas of interest are the house and the murder. Why was a man murdered? And did Dr. Fulthorpe know him? Dr. Fulthorpe needs to be contacted, especially now that his estate has been damaged. We'll need to see the fire marshal's report on whether they rule the blaze as arson, and if it is, the motive will have to be determined."

"Do we go back to talk to Dr. Crawford?" I said. "And see if Dr. Fulthorpe has returned to work yet?"

"We can try to speak with him. This has become a full-on criminal investigation. Dr. Fulthorpe will have some explaining to do and a lot of questions to answer. His absence isn't helping his case, either."

"Hmm," escaped my lips as I remembered what Aram had said to me a while ago.

"What, June?"

"I thought that Aram, Dr. Hamid, had said Dr. Fulthorpe was a good guy."

"Good guy in what regard?"

"Well liked. Respected."

"He may well be. But often, you never really know people, until you see what their actions are." Patrick put down the pen. "The three outliers in this case, which have to be proven to be related and relevant, are the guy that knocked you over, your house break-in, and the prank calls. If they're not related, we have more than one open investigation. Meanwhile, it's vital to be wary. If you are being sought after for whatever reason, it would be wise to keep you out of sight and inaccessible as much as possible. Is that all right? Are you okay with this?"

"I won't lie. This is all unnerving."

"June, I will do everything I can to keep you out of harm's way."

His eyes glistened. I believed him and trusted what he said. I wanted to forget everything for the rest of the night. All I longed to do was go upstairs to the cozy loft.

"Patrick. Can we head upstairs?"

"I'd like nothing more." He scooped me out of the chair with no apparent effort. He made me believe I was featherlight even as he soared up the stairs, two at a time.

Chapter Twenty-Eight

The moon hovered over the skylight, illuminating Patrick's muscled back. The bed sheet draped over his waist, and he slept peacefully, unaware of how I secretly admired him. In silence, I reflected on his strength, intelligence, kindness, and how he made me feel. The natural intimacy between us remained unparalleled with any connection I'd ever had.

And then ugly thoughts barged in. Unwelcome images of the fire and bloody crime scene rattled around and refused to leave my mind. Anxiety about the possible impending danger gripped my insides. My heart rate increased on its own.

It was no use trying to get back to sleep. I shimmied off the bed and waited to see if Patrick stirred. He remained still. I grabbed my cell phone from the night table, then stepped barefoot down the stairs to the front room. I looked out of the window at the still, ashen grey yard, trees, and road. Not even a night critter scurried by.

I sat on the couch and checked my phone for emails. I tapped on the gallery app and played the video I had filmed around the fire scene. I watched the dark, pixelated footage again and again—neighborhood houses, sidewalks, trees, shrubs, flashing lights, emergency vehicles. At the end of the video, a black car drove slowly by. A car. I scrolled in reverse. It looked like a luxury-size car, and the driver was a single shadowy occupant. Funny how I hadn't noticed it drive by at the time. I'd been so focused on the properties. Other than that, there was nothing to see. Patrick had been too kind to tell me my video recording would probably be a waste of time and effort. I hit delete.

I stood and peeked out the window one more time. A pair of headlights approached. I thought nothing of it until the car stopped at the end of the driveway. When the driver opened the door, my heart rate skyrocketed. A male figure got out, and I moved away from the window, pressing my spine against the wall. I stood frozen. A thump sounded at the front door, and I jumped. My pulse pounded in my ears, and for long seconds, I waited. A car door slammed, and I spied outside as the vehicle drove away.

On the porch sat a rolled-up newspaper.

"What are you doing?" Patrick said.

I leapt from the window. "I couldn't sleep. The newspaper is here."

"Thank you for letting me know that."

"Patrick, I thought the newspaper guy was a robber. Am I losing it?"

"You're not losing anything. What can I do to make you feel better? About all this?"

"You're already doing everything."

"Go on upstairs. I'll check everything is secure down here."

I went up to bed and realized I had left my phone on the couch. I retraced my steps down again. I checked for Patrick in the kitchen and front room, but I couldn't find him. Then I looked out the window. Outside, he bent over and picked up the newspaper. I expected him to come back in, but he didn't. Instead, he unrolled the newspaper and took out a slip of paper.

Was it a note? Tucked inside?

I turned and hurried upstairs and slipped back into bed. I pulled the bed sheet to my chin. My mind raced. What the heck was Patrick doing? Looking at some sort of coupon? Or a flyer? And why was it so interesting for him to want to read it in the middle of the night under the porch light?

Was it my imagination, or had he been acting secretively?

Chapter Twenty-Nine

At work, I sat in front of a computer monitor and stifled a yawn. Along with other things, Patrick's baffling rendezvous on the porch in the middle of the night got my mind reeling and robbed me of sleep. I was grateful Edward continued to train Ursula, giving me one less thing to do.

I leaned in when the DNA results from the now-scorched crime scene flashed onto the screen. I zoned in on the key items of the report.

Evidence Number: AA15843
Description: Ceiling tile
Type of evidence: Blood

DNA profile is consistent with a single source, major male profile, matching unknown major male from Evidence Number: AA15339.

To cross-check, I typed in AA15339.

Evidence Number: AA15339
Description: Swab from June Harber—left forearm
Type of evidence: Blood

Swab from June Harber—left forearm yielded a

DNA profile consistent from two sources, major female profile, June Harber, and one major male profile, identity unknown.

I sat back.

Though the identity of the "major male," my attacker, was still unknown, the DNA evidence placed him at the crime scene. He may have very well been the murderer himself.

My insides twisted. I had to tell Patrick. I grabbed my phone from my lab coat pocket and rushed toward the door. Lara looked at me as I whizzed by.

I dialed, and the call went to voicemail. "Hi, Patrick. I have an update on lab results. Talk to you soon."

Now I had two things to stress about—what Patrick had read on the porch and whether he'd been able to locate Dr. Fulthorpe. If he had located Dr. Fulthorpe, had he been able to question the doctor? My thoughts scattered in several directions. How had my simple life turned into a series of jumbled events?

Later, in the staff lounge, I downed the last drops of my tea. I still hadn't heard from Patrick. I paced the room in between the metal-bar sofa and the round laminate table. He was obviously busy working. He was a cop, for God's sake. Still, I remained impatient. I needed to talk about the case right now.

I exited the room and headed down the hallway. I trekked through the open doorway of Aram's office and found Ursula and Aram chatting. I stopped in my tracks. "Oh, excuse me." I shuffled my feet, trying to decide whether to stay or go.

"I'll see you later, Aram," Ursula said and all but blew him a kiss. She barely acknowledged me as she walked by.

Aram's face brightened with a smile. "It's wonderful to see you, June. How are you?"

"Fine, I think. Sorry about barging over here unannounced."

"Barge anytime."

Awkwardness diffused, and I smiled. "May I ask your opinion about something?"

"Of course," he said. "Would you like to shut the door?"

"Sure, that'd be best." I clicked it closed and perched on a chair. "Aram, I was just wondering, and I don't mean to be out of line, but I'd like to ask you something about Dr. Fulthorpe."

"Oh, yes, Stan Fulthorpe. But I don't know how much help I'll be. What would you like to know?"

"From the circles you run in, have you, by any chance, heard if he's back in town?"

"I have no idea. Why do you ask?"

"Police have confirmed his rental house burned down last night."

"That's horrible," Aram said. "Did anyone get injured?"

"No. It was vacant at the time."

"That's good. I hope Stan's insurance policy is up to date."

"Right," I said. "I never thought of that, but yes, for his sake I hope it is." I wondered if Dr. Fulthorpe could have been capable of arson for an insurance payout. There were so many variables to consider. "Sorry to have bothered you, Aram." I turned to leave.

"June."

I stopped.

"Would you like to tell me what you're not saying?"

His aqua eyes probed like a mesmerizing laser. "Am I that transparent?" My voice was almost a whisper. "Even after all this time?"

"I've studied everything about you, June, that is, when we were together. I haven't forgotten. Your forehead is creased, ever so slightly, but I notice it. And when you bit your bottom lip, I sensed there was something troubling you."

My frame became less stable.

"Did I just creep you out? You know I've done that before. Like the time I showed up when you were out with your friends."

I winced. "Oh, you definitely creeped me out when I saw you across the street. But now I know you're harmless. I mean, you wouldn't do me harm, intentionally." I had to stop reminiscing. We needed to focus on the reason I had come here. "You are right, Aram. There is something else I wanted to tell you. I think it'd be okay legally if I did."

"It'll go no further."

I didn't doubt he'd keep things silent.

"Here it goes," I said. "The house fire I just told you about. You've been there."

"I have?" He squinted. "Where was that?"

"The crime scene we examined with Officer Verbeek."

"That murder had occurred on Stan Fulthorpe's property?" Aram's demeanor darkened like a brewing storm. "How the hell did that happen?"

I shrugged.

"Let's see what Stan has to say." Aram picked up the phone and dialed. "Hematology clinic."

My mouth fell open, and I snapped it shut.

"Hello, it's Dr. Hamid calling from forensics. I'd like to speak with Dr. Fulthorpe."

I dared not move while eavesdropping.

"Do you know for how long?" He listened for a few moments. "No, it's fine. I'll catch him when he returns." He hung up.

"He's still away?" I stated the obvious. "For how long?"

"The receptionist didn't know. She was going to pass the phone to Dr. Crawford, but I dodged that."

"Phew," I said, and he smiled at me in that familiar way. My mouth went dry. "Well, thank you for your help, Aram. I have to get back to work."

In the afternoon I performed maintenance on one of the analyzers. I cleaned the internal surfaces, laser reader, probes, calibrated, and topped up solutions. Not unlike a machine, I worked on autopilot. My thoughts circulated around the case, Aram, and Patrick's inconsistent behavior. Why was he up last night to get the early morning paper? Was it for covert police work? Or could he be a dirty cop or an informant of some sort? Or was he cheating? These possibilities scared me more than any danger from the case.

Near quitting time, I checked my phone for messages. Patrick sent a kiss emoji, and I smiled. He was working late, and I'd have to cab it home.

I received a text from Debra, the flight attendant who lived above me at my duplex apartment.

—June, just letting you know a package arrived for you. I put it in the vestibule. And a heads-up, I hid the key to the basement door under the mat. I'm off for an overseas flight. Be back in a couple.—

A package? I didn't recall having ordered anything. It was still daylight; I'd swing by and get it.

I'd be in and out and steer clear of the basement.

Chapter Thirty

Along the drive to my duplex, I absently looked out of the taxi window. I appreciated how Aram had called Dr. Fulthorpe's office earlier and his diligence in working on the case. He was going above and beyond. He behaved like a knight in shining armor. I'd seen him act like this before.

I paid the driver and got out. My duplex house appeared quiet, tall, and almost unfamiliar, even though I hadn't been moved out for very long. I climbed the porch stairs, entered the vestibule, and saw a square box the size of a toaster. There was a typed label with my name on it, but no return address. I unlocked my apartment door and went inside. Everything appeared how I had left it, including the hallway floor that needed a good mopping.

I put my purse and the package down and grabbed a pair of scissors from the kitchen. The inner blade easily split the taped seam, and I unfolded the flaps. The box was filled with shredded newspaper. I put my hand in, fished around, and found something hard and flat. I pulled out a pink plastic hand mirror with cracks through it. A shard fell out, and I glanced at my cut-up, mosaic-like reflection. I found a note in the box with black marker printing.

How do you like your new face?

I dropped the mirror back into the box as if it was hot coal.

What kind of sick gesture was this?

Anger pulsed at my temples—a switch from being afraid all the time.

Whoever sent the box had mailed it, so they obviously stayed clear of my place. Coward!

Regardless of the louse staying away, I had to make sure my doors and windows weren't untampered with. As per Patrick's instructions, I grabbed the gun from my purse. It weighed heavy and solid like a dumbbell, and I cupped my other hand underneath, pointing it downward.

My heart thumped as I inspected each room, window, and the back door. There were no signs of entry or tampering that I could see. At this point, I was more nervous holding a loaded weapon than searching for a potential intruder. I went outside to check the backyard and crept downstairs to the basement. I took the key from underneath the mat but found the door ajar. Debra had been doing laundry down here sometime today before she left. She was probably in a rush and had not clicked the door shut.

Still pissed off, I kicked the door open and gripped the gun handle tighter. I peeked inside. Scant light filtered in, and the basement remained dingy and cluttered—nothing unusual. I entered and switched on the light.

Something moved in the back of the room, by a stack of plastic storage bins. That was no spider or centipede.

My heart picked up to a turbo pace, and pumping blood whooshed in my ears. Should I turn and run? But my feet wouldn't move. I lifted my arms and pointed the gun.

"Who's there?"

There was a dragging sound. Something or someone was behind a stack of boxes. My heart was about to burst from my chest.

"I have a gun!"

"Don't shoot," a male voice said.

I panted. My whole body shook. Senses overloaded my brain. I didn't know what to do. Run. Scream. I curled my finger over the trigger. "Who are you? Why did you leave me that package?"

"Package?"

"Who are you?"

He slowly stood from behind the boxes and held up his hands.

"You're him!"

His black clothes blended in with the shadows. "I'm not here to hurt you." His words were weak and slurred. Was he high? He shifted.

"Stay still!"

"Please, let—"

"Stop!" I yelled, but he wouldn't stand still and swayed forward. I couldn't let him get any closer, and I fired a warning shot to the far right. The man fell back.

As if someone was squeezing my throat, I struggled to breathe. Had I just shot him? But I hadn't been aiming at him. The shot should have missed him by a mile. Oh, God! His feet moved, and he groaned. I moved cautiously toward him with my gun still drawn. He held his shoulder with bloody fingers and looked at me with glassy eyes.

"Danger." The word escaped quietly from his

mouth, and he slumped back.

"Oh, God." I placed the gun on the ground and grabbed a T-shirt from the top of the dryer. I balled it up, but I was terrified to move closer to the man. He was breathing funny, labored, and he appeared to be in rough shape. I stepped closer. When I was in arm's length, I crouched, watching him the whole time. I bit my lip. I wasn't a doctor or a nurse. I had chosen to work in a lab because I didn't want to have patient contact—too squeamish. But here I was, attempting to do first aid. I slowly moved the guy's cool hand and pushed the cloth onto the wound.

He mumbled something I couldn't understand. Maybe I was hurting him, but I maintained pressure.

I grabbed my phone from my back pocket and struggled to hold it steady as I dialed.

"I need an ambulance," I said and recited my address.

"What's the emergency?" the attendant said.

"A man has been shot."

"Is he conscious?"

The man lay motionless. "I don't think so."

"Is he still breathing?"

His chest moved.

"Yes, he's breathing."

"Help is on the way. Are you able to apply pressure to the wound?"

"Yes. I am. Please hurry."

I hung up and dialed Patrick's number.

"Hey, babe," he said.

"I shot someone," I uttered as I looked at the guy's face. He didn't seem like a substance misuser. Sobs shook me from the inside out.

"What? Where are you?"

"At my apartment. The basement."

"Jesus! Are you hurt?"

"No."

"I'll be right there."

I hung up, and the phone jumped out of my hand.

The guy mumbled incoherently again. Clearly seeing his face now, this was the guy who had knocked me down that day. He opened his eyes.

My arm shook from maintaining pressure on the wound. "Who are you?"

"Dave," he said weakly and seemed completely nonthreatening.

"Dave, hang in there. An ambulance is on the way."

He closed his eyes.

Blood soaked through the T-shirt, but I kept holding it to the wound. He appeared to be out of it again. Seconds felt like hours. I sniffed. Tears pooled in my unblinking eyes. What had I done?

Finally. Sirens.

Suddenly, time sped up. A couple of male uniformed paramedics entered the basement. Black shiny boots stepped beside me, but I kept pushing on the saturated cloth.

"Hi, I'm Will, and this is my partner, Alex," the taller attendant said and crouched. He had a crew cut and wore a kind expression that touched my soul. "Can you tell me what happened?"

"I shot him," I said. "He's an intruder."

He pulled on gloves. "What's your name?"

"June. June Harber."

The other medic, I forgot his name, had a colorful tattoo of an autumn tree on his forearm. I wondered what it signified. He turned his lips up slightly and spoke in a comforting tone. "June, we can take over now."

"Oh, okay." I backed away and watched.

Will had already opened his case, removed scissors, and cut away the injured man's hoodie. He opened a package and applied a compression dressing.

The paramedic with the tattoo jumped in and took a blood pressure reading. "BP's low. Starting an IV."

I watched in horror. The real-life horror I'd created. If only this wasn't real. A bad dream I'd yet to wake from. Please let it not be real.

The door slammed open. Patrick. He came over and put his arms around me. I leaned against him, realizing how shaky my legs were.

"Are you all right?"

"Yes. No."

He rubbed my back in reassurance. "I'm just going to speak with the attendants."

The exchange of words barely registered in my head as I looked down. I opened and closed my hand.

"June, can you tell me what happened?" Patrick asked. "What is it?"

"My hand is sticky," I said.

He looked at my palm and fingers. "Let's get you upstairs."

In the bathroom, I pumped a handful of foam onto my bloodstained hands. I scrubbed vigorously and rinsed long after the red bubbles were gone. I thoroughly dried in between my fingers.

Patrick waited patiently and escorted me to the couch. "You're shaking."

"Don't worry. I'm getting used to it," I said in an attempt at humor.

"Let me make you a tea, and we'll sit for a bit."

"Thank you," I said, feeling like I was out of my body.

Soon he returned holding a mug. "There's no milk. Is black okay, or do you have some powdered creamer?"

"Black is fine," I said.

More emergency vehicles arrived and flashed outside the front window. Paramedics wheeled the stretcher with Dave on it into the ambulance. I shuddered.

"I bet the neighbors are wondering what happened," I said.

"Don't worry about the neighbors. June, was that the man who assaulted you?"

"Yes."

"Well, he is in custody now. And you are safe."

"Safe." I took a deep breath. "Am I really?"

"Come here." He put his arms around me.

"I don't know why he was here. And why he sent me that box, though he denied it."

"What box?"

I pointed to the cardboard box on the coffee table.

He looked at the mirror inside but didn't touch it. "He sent you this?"

"I'm assuming," I said.

"I'll submit it for prints," Patrick said.

A police officer came into the living room. "We removed a few personal items before they took the victim to the hospital." He glanced at me and then at Patrick.

"It's okay. She's helping with the investigation," Patrick said.

The officer handed Patrick a plastic ziplock bag.

Patrick emptied the contents onto the coffee table. A wallet, pill vial, lighter, and my long-lost work ID. My stomach constricted.

"My badge. He had it the whole time. But why was he after me? I never saw him kill anyone."

"Maybe he doesn't know that. It'll be in his best interest to cooperate and explain why he did what he did." Patrick opened the suspect's wallet and removed his driver's license. "His name is David Moreno."

My stomach churned, and bile rose. I bolted for the bathroom and expelled the scant contents of my stomach. I hunched over the sink and splashed cold water on my face. I stopped dousing and froze. Water dripped off my skin, and a paralyzing realization seeped through me.

I may have fired a lethal shot.

Chapter Thirty-One

"June?" Patrick's reflection frowned in the bathroom mirror.

I grabbed a towel and dabbed my face.

"How about we go to my place?" he said.

"Have you heard anything about David's condition?"

"No, but they're taking him to St. Eugene's Hospital. There will be an armed guard at his door."

"That's good," I said.

"It's protocol."

"Oh, right," I said, still not feeling reassured.

On the drive to Patrick's house, I stared straight ahead, reliving what had happened. Breath after breath, I struggled to draw in air.

Patrick pulled over to the side of the road.

"June, talk to me."

Traffic whizzed by, but Patrick didn't seem to care. He focused on me.

"David Moreno," I said, trembling, but not from being cold. "What if he dies?"

"We'll have to wait and see how he fares."

I shook my head. "I can't. I won't be able to sleep. Eat. I may have committed murder."

"He was alive when the paramedics took him. If he does, by chance, pass away, your reaction was in self-defense."

"I can't reconcile with having killed someone."

"You will, if you have to."

"I can't stand feeling like this. I need something. A tranquilizer."

"No, you don't."

"I do. Just one. I'll call my doctor."

"June, no."

"Please don't tell me no. You don't know what it's like for me to picture that pale, unarmed man crumple because of what I did."

Patrick rubbed his forehead. His brows were heavy.

"You do know."

"Not everything goes according to plan. Unfortunately."

"I'm sorry, Patrick."

"June, you are one of the most caring and sensitive people I've ever met. Try to stop flagellating yourself."

"I don't know how not to. The guilt is consuming me."

"How about we find out how David Moreno is doing. Right now. Are you up for a detour?" Patrick asked.

"To St. Eugene's?"

"Yes."

"I'd rather not." And then I thought more about it. I needed to know how David was doing. No matter what his crimes were, I didn't think I could deal with being responsible for taking a life, unless he had been charging at me with a weapon. But on the flip side, if he recovered, after I'd been afraid for so long, I wanted to make sure they secured him in custody. "If we go to the hospital, we wouldn't actually see him, right? We'll just ask at the front desk?"

"Whatever you're comfortable with."

"Okay. I changed my mind. I'm in."

"I'll be with you all the way."

I sighed. "I don't think you know how much that means to me."

He kissed the back of my hand. "Let's get this done."

He merged into traffic and parked at the hospital in the reserved emergency vehicle area. We entered through automatic doors and proceeded to the long information counter. The receptionist behind it had large brown eyes and had her hair pulled back into a knot at the base of her neck. She put down her cell phone when she noticed us. Patrick introduced who we were and inquired about the new admission, David Moreno. The clerk typed into her computer with long brown, almond-shaped nails.

"I'm sorry, his status is confidential."

"Can you tell us if he is alive or deceased?" I asked.

She shook her head. "I'm sorry, I can't."

There was a numbness inside of me at the lack of information. Patrick and I turned to leave.

"Excuse me," the receptionist said. "Because of the status of this patient's admission, I cannot divulge information here. But you are more than welcome to go up to the fifth floor and talk to the doctors there."

Patrick raised his brows and waited for my decision. I nodded.

We waited for the elevator. I blinked and felt a pinprick in my eye. I rubbed it but it continued to jab.

"Eyelash?"

"Yeah."

He crouched. "I can't see anything."

My eye watered, and the pain speared.

"There's a washroom near the coffee shop," I said. "I'll be right back."

In the ladies' room, I moved close to the mirror and found the culprit under my lower lid. I tapped on it and coaxed it out. Gone and done. The door flew open. Victoria. I froze in shock. Her eyes widened in surprise, but I was sure I looked absolutely stunned. My heart beat like a bass drum.

"What are you doing here?" she asked.

Still blunt as ever.

"Visiting," I said. She wore a uniform and a name badge. "Wait, are you working here again?"

"Yup. I'm back from wrongful termination," she said with attitude.

"That's just super." The union must have won her case. She slammed the hand dryer button as I walked out. I shook my head. The best thing I did was leave my job at this hospital.

Patrick paced at the elevator.

"Everything all right?" he asked.

"You won't believe who I ran in to."

"Who's that?"

"Victoria Silverstone."

"Your fired ex co-worker?"

"Yes. But I found out she has been unfired."

"What?"

"You heard me."

"She probably got off on a technicality," he said.

"Yeah."

The elevator bell dinged. The door opened, and an older gentleman with a cane got off.

"Are you sure you want to go up?"

"Maybe," I said but stepped into the elevator, anyway. On the fifth floor, a hospital-specific smell lingered in the air—a combination of bodily outputs, antiseptics, and other artificial fragrances. It reminded me how grateful I was to work in a well-ventilated lab where I could deal with smelly specimens in a fume hood. We walked halfway down the beige tiled hall to the nurse's station. The chairs by computer terminals were all empty. At the very end of the corridor, a uniformed police officer sat on a chair outside a door. Patrick and I glanced at each other.

"He must be in there," I said.

"Are you ready to find out?"

I nodded. There was no backing out now.

I followed a step behind Patrick to the last room. The other officer stood up from his chair.

"Good evening, Officer," Patrick said.

"Hello." The shorter man straightened and adjusted his utility belt.

"I'm Patrick Verbeek, and this is June Harber from forensics." Patrick showed his badge to the fellow.

"Yes, I recognize you. Chad Griffin."

"Oh, right. You were on the Marine Unit. Good to see you."

"You, too. What can I do for you?"

"I'm investigating a case. Is David Moreno in there?"

"He is. They just brought him up from the ER."

"Is he being cooperative?" Patrick asked.

"Not at the moment. He's in a coma."

"Coma?" I squeaked out of my tight throat. As Patrick and the guard talked, I peeked into David's room.

Lights flashed on several monitors. His pale face looked serene, and his limp arms rested on top of the bedsheet. A bag of IV fluid and a pint of blood hung on a pole beside him, each hooked up to an arm. Unmoving and quiet, he seemed benign, unthreatening. Not the attacker I had feared for so many days and nights. I backed away, ready to leave. Ready to put all this behind me. I realized how weary I had become. My body had become leaden.

"I'll come by tomorrow," Patrick said to the guard. "Maybe I'll be able to question him then."

"Sure, Officer. I'll leave word."

A woman in navy scrubs pushed a large instrument on wheels. "I'm here from x-ray. Can I go in?" she said to the group of us.

"Go ahead," the guard said.

Patrick and I retraced our way down the hallway. I felt no closure or comfort knowing this guy was under complete surveillance. Nor could I shake the sick feeling that he was comatose because of me. We waited for the elevator.

"I feel like an executioner," I said.

"You're not, babe. Let's call it a night and question him tomorrow."

Choked up with emotion, all I could muster was a nod.

****

The next morning, I struggled to lift my head off the pillow. Patrick was already dressed.

"You tossed and turned all night."

"I did?" I held back a yawn.

"I have something urgent to tend to. How about you stay home from work and rest?" he said.

"I'll be fine once I get going."

He came over and kissed me. "Sure?"

"Positive."

"Okay then. I'll talk to you soon." He gave me a final kiss and left.

I dragged myself out of bed and got ready. Numbness crept into my brain. Numbness could be good.

I was the last to arrive at work, and Vinny and Edward looked up.

Lara rushed over. "Patrick just called us and told us what happened. Are you okay? It must have been terrifying to find that prowler in your basement," she said.

Tears pooled in my eyes. I nodded. "It was." My brain neurons were struggling to fire. "How's the backlog?"

"Same old, same old," Vinny said.

"You have dark circles under your eyes," Lara said.

"I do?" I buttoned up my lab coat.

"I'm worried about you," Lara whispered.

"I'm fine, really. Do you want me to take the fridge temperatures?" I said and opened the door to the hot air oven.

Lara and Edward looked at each other, and I'd realized what I'd done.

"How about you take some time off, June," Edward said.

I opened my mouth to object but stopped. It was a valid suggestion. "Okay."

"Take all the time you need," Lara said. "Oh, just to let you know, Dr. Hamid came in looking for you."

"Thanks for everything, Lara. I'll talk to you soon."

"Take care," Ursula said as I walked by.

I smiled slightly at her gesture of kindness. "Thank

you, Ursula."

No one passed me in the corridor as I made my way to Dr. Hamid's office. His door was pulled closed but not clicked shut. I knocked lightly.

"Come in," he said. He sat, posture straight, at his microscope and then rolled his chair back.

"Good morning," he said. His smile disappeared. "What's the matter?"

I dropped into a chair, spent, as if I had fought fifteen rounds.

He jumped up and shut the door. He sat beside me and put a gentle hand on my knee. "What happened?"

I was acutely aware of his touch, but I believed his gesture was of sincere concern. I told him everything that had occurred the day before with David Moreno.

"June, you did nothing wrong."

"But I did. I pulled a trigger. And now a man is in a coma. Well, he was in a coma last night. I don't know his status today."

"You said he sustained a shoulder injury?"

"Yes."

"Those wounds are usually not fatal. He should be better with fluids and antibiotics. If it's an infection he's fighting."

"The not knowing and waiting is so hard."

Aram turned to his desk drawer and pulled out a coconut-filled chocolate bar.

Way back when, he'd given me this particular treat whenever I was having a challenging day.

"A Tropical Delight," I said. "I haven't had one of these since…" I stopped myself from finishing the sentence. "Thank you, Aram."

"You're welcome. Now, let's put your mind at rest

and see how Mr. Moreno is doing this morning." Aram awakened his computer screen and logged into St. Eugene's Hospital portal. He typed in the name, and the file came up. He scrolled down the series of results and reports and read them out loud.

"Single gunshot, left posterior shoulder."

"Wait. Posterior?"

"Yes, that's what it says."

How had my bullet hit him in the back? Had it ricocheted?

Aram kept reading. "Vitals are listed. And here are bloodwork reports. His hemoglobin is quite low," Aram said. "His D-Dimer is elevated—not a surprise from bleeding."

I listened intently.

"This is interesting," he said.

"What?"

"He has some renal dysfunction. His coagulation results are abnormal. Bleeding time is increased."

"No wonder he was bleeding so much." I watched the screen as Aram scrolled. "Is there a history?"

Aram clicked on a few tabs. "Yes, there is. Von Willebrand's disease."

"Von Willebrand's?" I said. "He sounds like a sick man."

"Yeah, I'd say he isn't well. And he is being treated at the hematology clinic at St. Eugene's," Aram said.

My ears perked up. "Who is the specialist?"

"Dr. Fulthorpe."

"They know each other? This can't be a coincidence. They are connected in all of this somehow," I said.

"I agree with you. And speaking of another

connection. You'll never guess who called me."

"Who?"

"Dr. Gideon Crawford. The receptionist had told him I had called looking for Dr. Fulthorpe. He said Dr. Fulthorpe was away and asked if he could assist me instead."

"What did you say?"

"I divulged nothing. I said I was just wondering if Stan Fulthorpe was still out of town."

"It was nice of Dr. Crawford to follow up." I backed away from the monitor. "And I think this information about David Moreno will be helpful. Thank you for searching for the results."

"Of course, June. That's what I'm here for."

"I'm going to update Patrick," I said.

"You definitely should do that." He bowed his head. "So, June, you and the officer, you're getting along well?"

Why had Aram asked about my relationship with Patrick? Was it out of curiosity? Or was Aram showing interest in something else? With us? A rekindling? Whatever the reason, it wouldn't change a thing with Patrick and me.

"Yes, we're getting along well."

"I'm glad you're happy," he said with what sounded like sincerity.

But was he *really* happy?

Chapter Thirty-Two

I closed my locker and called Patrick. It went to voicemail.

"Hi, I'm just letting you know I'm taking the rest of the day off. I should have listened to you earlier. Talk to you soon."

I phoned for a taxi and waited outside at the curb. I pulled on the hood of my jacket, but no matter which way I turned, the wind blew in my face. Traffic whooshed by as I watched for my cab and took glimpses of my phone.

Patrick. Call. Make sense of all this for me. Please.

If David was shot from behind, why was he bleeding from the front? Could the report have had an error?

My phone vibrated, and I quickly answered. "Hello?"

"This is Larry's Garage. I'm looking for June Harber."

Traffic whizzed by, and I put my free hand to my ear. "Yes, speaking."

"Your car is ready for pickup. Do you know when you'll be here? We're open 'til five."

"That is great news," I said. "I will be there soon."

A taxi slowed in front of me. I waved and climbed in.

"Larry's Garage on Main Street, please," I said to the unshaven driver.

The pine deodorizer hanging from the rearview mirror failed to mask the odor of either a skunk or cannabis. I cracked open the window and hoped the driver wasn't high. Along the way, I clutched my cell phone in my hand. The cabbie pulled into the car repair lot, and I paid him. I entered the shop's compact front office. Dank smells of engine oil hung in the air. A mechanic in blue coveralls came over to the counter.

"Hi, I'm June Harber. Here to pick up my car."

He grabbed the paperwork from a file folder and read the report. "Oh, yes. We found sludge in the gas tank and in the engine. It was a royal mess."

"Really?" I didn't know what to have expected, but it wasn't that.

"We had to do a complete engine check, flushed the intakes, and replaced the gas tank. Sorry about the delay, but the tank took a long time getting here. Your total with tax is at the bottom." He turned the paper around and slid it toward me.

I gulped and fished a credit card from my wallet. "What could have caused all this damage?"

The guy scratched his weathered forehead with a black thumb. "Something caustic and sugary was poured into the gas tank. Perhaps you should get a locking gas cap. Should run fine now. Come back if you have any problems." He handed me the key.

"Thank you," I said and went outside.

Finally, I could drive my old familiar car. Unfortunately, the repairs may have cost more than the car was worth. Who in the hell would do such a thing? And then I thought of David Moreno. Could he have done it? Most likely. But why? When he was conscious, I'd hand him my car repair bill.

I still needed answers about David's injury and how I had caused it with my warning shot. I couldn't wait any longer for Patrick to call.

I drove to St. Eugene's Hospital and parked in the front lot. Some of Patrick's gumption was rubbing off on me. I switched off the ignition, clipped my work badge onto my collar, and marched inside. I prepared mentally. My plan would be to go in and ask to speak with the nurse caring for David. Certainly, she would know the nature of the wound since she was dressing it. I moved through the lobby and rode the elevator to the fifth floor, retracing the steps I took with Patrick the day before. At the end of the hall, as expected, I saw a police officer sitting outside the room on a chair. He had a smooth face, fine lips, and prominent cheekbones—a different guy from the day before.

I took a controlled breath. I couldn't believe I was doing this.

"Hello, Officer…"

"Evans," he said and stood.

"Officer Evans." I said, trying to sound like I belonged there. "I'm June Harber, forensic scientist on this case."

"It didn't take long for you to get here," he said.

"Take long? How do you mean?"

"Moreno's regained consciousness."

"Ah, yes, of course," I said, acting like I knew. The lie didn't sit well with me. "Have you seen David's nurse recently?" I was relieved David had awakened, but his alertness created a whole new scenario. I hadn't expected to have to actually speak with him. My mind reeled. Would he recognize me? And what would he say if he did? "I have a question to ask his nurse."

"You're in luck. She is in there with the doctor. You can go right in."

My heartbeat drummed in my ears. My simple plan instantly became complicated. Should I enter the room or make an excuse to leave?

"Okay, thank you," I said and pushed open the door. The decision was made, but what the devil was I doing? I had crossed boundaries. I didn't do stuff like this. With trepidation, I entered quietly and froze in place. The nurse and doctor hadn't noticed me yet.

"Have you checked his personal possessions? Is it in his wallet?" The doctor opened the locker at the side of the room. And then I recognized him, and his cologne. It was Dr. Crawford, Dr. Fulthorpe's partner.

"He didn't arrive with any personal possessions," the nurse said. "I just gave him the pain meds you prescribed. If he wakes up again, I'll ask him what medications he's taking."

Dr. Crawford shut the locker. "Let's repeat his bloodwork before we give him another unit of blood." He looked at me before he walked out. I thought there was a moment of recognition, but perhaps he couldn't quite place seeing me from the other day.

"Can I help you?" the nurse said.

"I'm June Harber with forensics. I have a quick question, if that's okay?"

I glanced at David. His eyes were closed.

"The doctor just walked out; do you want to speak with him instead?"

"I'm sure you can help," I blurted out.

"I'll try," she said and took off her glasses, leaving them to hang on a chain around her neck.

"I appreciate that, thanks. I'd like to ask about Mr.

Moreno's shoulder wound. Could you tell me, was he shot anteriorly or posteriorly?"

"I can tell you the nastiest injury is in the front," she said.

My stomach twisted. My tiniest bit of consolation to shooting an unarmed man was I hadn't meant to actually hit him. I had to reconcile with the fact of what I had done.

"Excuse me, one other thing," I said. "Do you mind me asking what Dr. Crawford wanted with his personal possessions?"

"He was looking for a medications list."

"Oh," I said. "I actually saw his personal items the other day, before the ambulance brought him here, and I didn't see a list, just to let you know."

I heard a rustling sound from the bed.

The nurse bustled over to him. "Are you in pain, David?"

He cracked his eyes open. "Need mem-mory," he mumbled.

"We have given you morphine, David. You'll remember things just fine later. Try to rest," she said.

He became still again. His face relaxed in slumber.

"He's out cold," I said.

"Dr. Crawford prescribed enough morphine to knock out an elephant. He'll have a good sleep." The nurse checked the IV infusion pump.

"Thank you for your help."

"You're welcome."

When I arrived at Patrick's place, I couldn't recall the drive. I dropped my handbag in the doorway and trudged through the house, removing my clothes as I walked, and leaving them where they landed. Upstairs, I turned on the shower and let the hot water consume me until I couldn't tolerate the heat anymore. I shut the water off and stepped out of the stall, but no bath towel hung on the rack. Like a wet duck, I plodded into the bedroom. I crawled under the covers on Patrick's side of the bed. His scent soothed better than any essential oil.

Rest. I needed rest.

The worst was over.

Everything would be okay.

Chapter Thirty-Three

My mobile phone rang, and it startled me awake. I pushed damp hair out of my eyes and groped the bedsheets for my phone.

"Hey, Patrick," I said sleepily.

"How are you doing?"

"I'm all right, just had a nap." I heard repeated tapping. "Are you running?"

"Yeah. Jogging to my car," he said. "Can you be ready to go out in an hour?"

"Yes. Is something going on?"

"Nothing to worry about."

"Are you sure?"

"Yes, sure. I'll fill you in when I see you. Trust me, babe."

"I trust you."

I dropped my head back onto the pillow. Where was Patrick going to take me? It'd give me a chance to fill him in on my earlier escapade at the hospital.

I couldn't figure out Dr. Crawford's rationale for searching for David Moreno's medication list. Why would he need it? He could easily do bloodwork and treat David as needed. And he and Dr. Fulthorpe shared a practice. I assumed they could access each other's files. It would be easy for Dr. Crawford to find out what meds David was on.

I had to get moving and threw off the covers. Less than perfectly, I made the bed and dressed in black yoga pants and a sage tunic. After brushing, I clipped my hair into a ponytail. I took Patrick's computer from the night table, leaned against the headboard, and turned it on. I had enough time for a quick browse before he showed up.

I clicked on the file containing the saved names from the flash drive and wondered if David Moreno's name was on the list. Not that I would know the significance of it, even if it appeared. I scrolled down in expectation, wanting to call Bingo. But page after page, I found no matches. No win for this idea.

From the icons on the screen, I chose the solitaire game and started moving cards around. I transferred a red onto a black, a black onto red. I lost interest in playing as my mind drifted.

Patient ID numbers. Answers had to be with those patient ID numbers.

Why were these names on a stick? Who were they? Why would someone put a flash stick in the ceiling? Did it belong to my landlord? As far as I knew, he was a retired lawyer. Maybe it was his. I didn't think he'd mind if I called him.

I checked the directory in my phone and dialed. It rang twice, and he answered.

"Hello?"

"Hi, Mr. Sutton. It's June Harber. How are you?"

"Fine, but we'll be doing better once we can get away to Vermont. The police came by to tell us what had happened and asked several questions. How are you?"

"I'm doing better, thanks. Sorry to bother you, but I have yet another question to ask you, too, if you don't mind. It may seem like an odd one."

"Sure."

"A couple of weeks ago, I found a flash drive in the basement."

"A what?"

"A flash drive. A USB memory stick for the computer. It was tucked up in the ceiling."

"You don't say."

"I was wondering if it was yours? I thought perhaps you used it for work?"

"I've been retired for some time. I've never used those devices. All my records were in paper files, locked at my office, or on the computer hard drive."

"So, it's not yours?"

"No, not mine."

"Do you have any idea who it could belong to?"

"Maybe it belongs to Debra upstairs. Or perhaps it belonged to the fellow you found in the basement. We'll have to make the house more secure for you."

"Thank you, Mr. Sutton. I appreciate that. And I'll check with Debra. Enjoy Vermont." I hung up, but I seriously doubted it belonged to Debra. To be certain I would message her to ask.

An engine rumbled. I ran downstairs, peeked out and swung open the front door as Patrick stepped onto the porch. He wore jeans and a black raglan long-sleeved shirt.

"Hey," he said and slipped his arms around me. His lips touched mine in a supple sensuality that made my mind and body soar in tranquility.

"Hmm," I sighed. "Just what I needed."

"Are you feeling all right, June? I was worried when I saw your text."

I put my head against his chest. "Yes, much better."

He kissed the top of my head. "Sorry. This situation hasn't been easy on you."

"I just want it to be over."

"It will be. I promise."

"So, what are we doing?"

"Are you up for a drive?" Patrick asked.

"I am. Where to?"

"You'll see when we get there."

"Oh, great. Another mystery," I said, feigning annoyance.

"I guarantee you'll like this one."

Tingly inside, I smiled. "I'll get my purse." I picked up my bag. The weight of it was much lighter without the gun, which was still with the police unit. Ugg. Another reminder.

"I see you got your car back," Patrick said as we sat in his truck.

"Yes, finally."

"What was wrong with it?" While driving, he glanced over at me.

"It was a major repair. Someone had poured something into my gas tank."

He thumped the steering wheel with a fist.

"At this point, I guess there's nothing else you can do."

He shook his head. "Not much. But I will document it."

We drove on country roads, along fields of corn, tall and ready for the harvest. I tipped my head back into the headrest. The sway of the ride rocked and soothed. Maybe everything really would be resolved soon. Patrick took my hand, and I gave it a squeeze.

"So, Officer, are you going to keep me in suspense?"

"I thought we'd go for a bite on the outskirts of town. Have you heard of Lucy's Country Kitchen?" he asked.

"No, I haven't."

"I hope you like it. They have the best pies." He kissed the back of my hand.

I'd never tire of this.

He turned onto a main road. On the right, a large house had a wraparound porch and lights along the eaves. A fluorescent sign said Lucy's Country Kitchen. Patrick parked in the gravel lot and shut off the engine.

"Ready to go in?" he said.

"Yes."

But he placed a hand on my thigh to stop me from getting out. He put a finger to his lips and handed me a note.

Don't say anything. Leave your phone in the car.

My contentment bubble burst, and nerves prickled inside.

He told me not to talk, but that's all I wanted to do. Alarmed, I looked at him and mouthed the words, "what's going on?"

He pointed to the building. I nodded and left my phone under the seat. We got out of the vehicle and entered the diner. Patrick chose the booth in the back corner.

A middle-aged server dressed in black pants and a white blouse brought us a couple of glasses of water. The wet glasses soaked the paper place mat menus.

"I'll be back to take your order," she said.

When she left, I leaned forward. "What is going on?"

"With everything that has happened, I've been hesitating to fill you in on details about one of my previous cases. But for your safety, it's come to the point I have to. Also, there's been a new, sudden development in our case."

"Oh, wow." I took a sip of water. "Okay. Shoot."

"I'll start with a quick backstory. A few years ago, I was patrolling the streets and saw a young guy speeding in a purple Maserati. I immediately put on the sirens, but he wouldn't pull over. Thanks to construction, the chase led to a dead end. The arrogant young man called his rich dad, who offered a sizeable bribe to drop everything. But I said no to a guy who wasn't used to anyone saying no. I booked him for bribery and a few other charges. As I put on his cuffs, he asked if I had a wife and children, and said it would be a shame if I wasn't around to protect them. This guy doesn't have a history of being forgiving."

I shivered and rubbed my arms.

"He was released from prison earlier than expected and has been spotted in the area. We have to make certain my house, car, or our phones aren't being monitored. And when I'm not using it, I have to put my phone in an EMF blocking bag, so I'm not tracked."

"So that's why so many of my calls were going to voicemail. My God, Patrick."

"Try not to fret about it. This is precautionary. This guy has a list of enemies, and I may not even be near the top. The undercover team will keep me updated."

"Updated how? With a note in the morning newspaper?"

Patrick paused. "You knew about that?"

"The other night, when I couldn't sleep, I came back

downstairs and found you outside on the porch."

"And you didn't question me about it?"

I shook my head. "I didn't know what to think, so I said nothing."

"I'm sorry I wasn't forthcoming." He dipped his chin.

I shifted on the vinyl bench. My conscience alerted me not to be hypocritical. I was not without sin. I hadn't been forthcoming either about my past involvement with Aram. "Patrick, you don't have to apologize."

The waitress put a wire rack of condiments onto the table. I stopped talking until she was out of earshot.

"Has anything like this happened to you before? Being targeted?"

"I've had angry threats from guys I arrested, but none have followed through."

"I'm frightened for you."

"It's all part of law enforcement," he said and took a drink.

"Have you ever thought of taking up something else, like farming?"

He chuckled. "Actually, I have. You see where I live."

"Oh, wow. You're not kidding."

"Not at all."

The server came back with a pad of paper and pen. "Have you decided on your order?"

"Yes," I said and pointed to an item on the menu. "I'd like the Hamburg Deluxe special, please. And an iced tea."

"Make that two."

"No problem," the attendant said and retreated.

"I know little about police procedures, but I trust

you'll do what you need to do. To be safe. Right?"

"Yes, we're on it."

"Okay, good." I chewed on the side of my lip. "Patrick, I couldn't stop thinking about our case, and I went to the hospital this morning."

Patrick raised his eyebrows.

"I found out David Moreno is out of his coma. Have you had a chance to question him yet?"

"That's the other topic I wanted to discuss," he said.

"You did question him?"

"No, June, he couldn't talk."

"No? Was he still sleepy from the morphine? Or did he refuse?"

Patrick's jaw tightened. "June," he said quietly. "He's dead."

Blood drained out of my face. "Dead? How? Earlier today he was alive and stable." I tried to let the news register. "I killed him."

"June, listen to me. You didn't kill anyone. Ballistics will prove that. Please try to take a step back and wait for the loose ends of the case to be tied up."

"Ends are being tied up? As in, case closed?"

"It would appear that way. With David's DNA at the crime scene, we can conclude he's implicated in murder, or manslaughter. But, with David gone, and no other suspect, there can be no trial. Leads have run cold. So, it's case closed, as you put it."

"Except..." I said.

"Except what?"

"I don't know. I guess I should be relieved, but I can't believe this is all over."

"Believe it. Protocol dictates an autopsy must be performed on David Moreno because he passed away

193

within twenty-four hours of hospital admission. But after that, we should officially wrap things up."

I took a deep breath. "It'll be such a relief," I said. "But something is so weird, though."

"What is?"

"When David appeared in my basement, I was scared. Terrified, stiff. Beyond anything I'd ever felt. Thinking back, he didn't seem like a threat. I don't think he wanted to hurt me."

"Actions show how people truly are. Some people don't seem to be threatening until they reveal their claws and fangs."

"Like wolves in sheep's clothing."

"Exactly."

The server delivered a tray with our drinks and plates of fries and grilled burgers. The best smells I'd had all day. I picked up my iced tea in a toast. Though it was the most disparaging occasion I'd ever toasted to.

"Cheers, Patrick. To a case that seemed to solve itself."

Chapter Thirty-Four

The next morning, a couple of uniformed officers and electronic experts searched Patrick's house for bugs and hidden cameras. The threat against him from that other case was very real. I sidestepped the men several times as they scanned everything from the floorboards, furniture, lamps, to the ceilings and even the attic. At the front door, I gave Patrick a quick kiss before heading out to work.

Patrick kept hold of my hand. "I can't wait to get you back upstairs," he said.

An officer walked by us and scratched his shaved head. "Well, you'll have to wait a little longer. There's a crew in the bedroom."

Patrick chuckled, and my cheeks blew up in flames as I rushed out of the house.

In the lab, I stayed clear of the fume hood area, where there was tension between Ursula and Vinny. Ursula had contaminated some samples, and Vinny watched her pipetting technique as if she was a new grad. Her face glowed red, and her lips flattened as she pressed them together. I empathized. We'd all been humbled by the job at one time or another.

On the other side of the lab, I sat at a computer, evaluating results and writing reports. My mind wandered to my case. It wasn't over until it was over.

The death of David Moreno became a coroner's case, and Aram was performing the autopsy at this very moment. He had asked if I wanted to assist, but I declined. My attempt at assisting last time hadn't worked out so well, and attending the postmortem on David Moreno would certainly be more daunting.

The phone rang, and Edward answered. He waved me over.

"For me?"

"Yeah," Edward said and put the receiver on the bench top.

Who could be calling? Another prank? But David Moreno was dead. I stood and hesitated before walking over to pick up the telephone.

"Hello?" I said tentatively.

"June, it's Aram."

I let out a breath. "Oh, hi. What can I do for you, Dr. Hamid?"

"Could you come down to the autopsy suite? There is something here I think you'll want to see."

"Aram, I can't," I whispered.

"I completely understand, but I promise this won't take long, and, more importantly, it will answer some of your questions."

What could he be referring to? "Okay. I'll be right there."

"Heading to the morgue?" Edward said.

"Yes, is it all right if I leave for a bit?"

"Yeah. You better do what the doc wants," he said.

I nodded. "Right," I said, with no idea of what the doc really wanted.

My hand trembled as I pushed the elevator button to go down to the dreaded basement. I scanned my badge to get into the autopsy suit foyer and knocked on the door that was open a crack. Inside, Aram was fully dressed in a protective gown, gloves, and mask. He had been mindful enough to put a sheet over the body.

"Come in, June. I finished the examination, and I'll make this as quick as possible."

"I appreciate that," I said and also put on protective wear. The danger was over, but being here was still traumatizing. My chest constricted, and my heart hammered.

"Around here."

I walked around the gurney and put fingers to my forehead, ready to shield my face.

"I'm sorry. I thought this would be good closure for you. Would you prefer I show you photographs instead?"

"No, no. I'm good." My heart still pounded, but I didn't feel woozy like the last time.

"All right. Here it goes." He lifted the sheet to reveal David Moreno's shoulder wound. I stared at a crimson hole surrounded by jagged skin.

"Anterior wound," he said.

I couldn't speak.

"Now, I will show you the posterior wound." He rolled David over enough for me to see the back of his shoulder. There was a tiny round hole, no blood, barely noticeable. Aram carefully released David onto his back again.

I made eye contact with Aram. "He was hit twice?"

"No, June. Just once. Mr. Moreno was shot posteriorly."

"How could I have done that? Did the bullet ricochet off the concrete wall?"

"No, again. I won't get technical, but in a nutshell,

David Moreno was hit point blank. He received a bullet in the back that exited the front. See how the exit wound is larger, more irregular, and has an outward beveling of tissue? From where you were standing, the bullet couldn't have been from your gun."

I stepped back and exhaled the breath I was holding. My eyes welled up with moisture. "Whoa. You have no idea what a relief that is." A heavy burden dropped from my heart. "Wait, Aram. If I didn't shoot him, then who did?"

"Good question. My guess would be someone who had it out for him."

Beneath the still sheet lay a lifeless body, housing so many unrevealed secrets.

"June, could you meet me in my office later today? To go over the rest of the autopsy findings."

"Yes, of course." I backed away. I removed my personal protective equipment, washed my hands, and left the morgue area. Instead of returning to the lab, I made a beeline to the end of the hallway. I slammed the door open and burst outside. I leaned against the rough brick wall and gulped a lungful of fresh air. I hadn't killed David Moreno. I hadn't even injured him. In silent prayer, I closed my eyes and listened to wind gusts and rustling leaves. The crisp temperature invigorated me like a dunk in a glacial lake. The burden of guilt broke free from my soul.

David Moreno, I don't know what happened to you, but I'm going to do my best to find out.

I returned to work with a renewed purpose to find answers. I kept checking the time and shifted restlessly in my chair. I couldn't wait another second and went to Aram's office. When I arrived, his office was empty. I should have been more patient. I turned to retreat and saw him walking toward me. He smiled disarmingly, catching me off guard.

"Looking for me?" he said.

Busted. "Yes, I'm a bit early."

"Come in." We entered his office. He closed the door, pulled out a chair for me, and sat behind his desk. "How are you doing? Have you recovered from this morning?"

"I am enormously better now, knowing I wasn't responsible for David's death. Aram, I've been so self-absorbed through all of this. Thank you for always being so kind and for putting my mind at ease."

"You've never been self-absorbed. I'm glad to have helped."

I needed to keep this conversation focused on business. "So, what did you find during the autopsy? And please leave nothing out."

He leaned into his chair and crinkled his brow before he spoke. "Upon examination, it appeared David had a lot of internal bleeding. A distended abdomen, hemorrhagic areas around the organs, skin bruises."

"He was beat up?"

"He was likely assaulted, which wouldn't have caused the serious injuries he sustained if he didn't have a bleeding disorder. Any blunt force injury could be made one-hundred times worse."

"Von Willebrand's disease," I said.

"Yes, Von Willebrand's. It's more common than hemophilia, but less known about."

"Poor guy," I said. "And then he gets shot. Did he die from extreme blood loss?"

"June, that is the main reason I wanted to speak with

you. Because of his condition, and lack of medical care, David Moreno did indeed suffer severe blood loss. Yes, he was anemic, but the cause of death wasn't blood loss. It was a brain hemorrhage."

"Oh my God."

"I've taken representative samples from the brain, other organs, veins, arteries. Also, all fluids—urine, blood, eye. And I submitted a request for a toxicology screen as well."

"Is excessive bleeding the reason people with Von Willebrand's die? And so young?"

"It's possible, but cases like this aren't well documented."

"Aram, I appreciate how you always make time to help."

"Of course," he said.

I stood.

"Did you ever figure out who those people are on that flash drive?"

All this time, I'd been obsessing about who the drive belonged to. The only logical answer was David Moreno. He had hid it in my basement, and it appeared people were after him. But the next question was, what was its significance?

"No. I'm more curious than ever as to who those people are."

"I don't have time at this moment, but do you want me to have another look? I can search each number in the hospital database to see if they are actually patient ID numbers?"

"I'd be really interested to know that."

"Would you like to come to my place one evening and check it out together?"

"Your place?"

There was a knock on the door. I hesitated, then looked at Aram before I answered it. The distraction saved me from responding to his invitation. I opened the door. It was Ursula, with freshly applied lip gloss.

"Oh, you're here," she said.

"Yes, here I am," I said.

"There was a call for you. I left a note on your bench."

"I appreciate that, Ursula. I was just leaving. Aram, thank you for the preliminary autopsy report."

"You're welcome, June. We'll connect again when the bloodwork results have been completed."

"The sooner the better," I said. "Have a great evening."

I stepped out of the office and heard Ursula laughing in the distance. It was obvious she had her sights on Aram.

Who was I to criticize?

Chapter Thirty-Five

At my desk in the lab, I unfolded the scribbled message Ursula had left for me.

June,

Dr. Crawford called. Call him back.

I sat and swiveled to-and-fro on my chair. What could Dr. Crawford want with me?

Lara waved, wearing her trench coat with the strap of her handbag over her shoulder. "Earth to June."

"Sorry, Lara," I said. "Are you on your way home?"

"Yes, finally," she said. "You should get out of here, too. And get more rest. Promise?"

I smiled and crossed my heart.

Edward and Vinny were at the stainless-steel sink scrubbing their hands, getting ready to head out, too. "Night, June," they all said.

"Have a great weekend, everyone," I said. The door slammed shut, and all became quiet.

I sat holding the note, mulling over whether or not to call Dr. Crawford. I picked up the phone and dialed. A male voice answered.

"Hello, is Dr. Crawford there?"

"Speaking."

"Hi, this is June Harber."

"June, I appreciate you calling. I'll cut to the chase. I am concerned about my partner, Stan Fulthorpe. Do you know if Officer Verbeek has located him?"

"I'm sure if you speak with the officer, he'll give you an update."

"I will. I have another question. David Moreno's nurse told me you had seen his personal possessions. Is that true?"

"Yes, I did," I said. "I saw them before they were submitted for evidence. Why do you ask?" He couldn't be looking for David's medication list again. Could he?

"Can you tell me what the items were?"

I found it very odd how Crawford was talking to me about this matter. "I'm sorry. I don't think I'm the right person for you to be asking about this."

"I apologize I'm not following the proper protocols, but I'm concerned about my partner. Do you, by any chance, recall coming across Stan's private cell number?"

"Oh, I understand," I said and tried to remember all the items the police had retrieved from David's pockets that day at my duplex. "I remember there was an empty pill vial and a wallet. They're in police evidence." I didn't tell Dr. Crawford that David also had my ID badge; I didn't want to explain that aspect.

"Can you recall any other item? A ball bead keychain?" Dr. Crawford said.

"There weren't any keys," I said and noted that was a specific detail he asked about.

"Thanks for your help anyway," he said, sounding disappointed. "How are you doing, June? I heard Moreno broke into your house the day before he passed away."

How could he know that? "I'm fine," I said. "How did you come across that information?"

"I spoke with Dr. Hamid in consultation about the

case."

I exhaled. "I see. I will be sure to mention I talked with you to Officer Verbeek."

I hung up and went to my locker. My cell phone rang, and I grabbed it from my purse.

"Hey, Patrick."

"Hi, babe. I have a lead on finding Dr. Fulthorpe, so I'm going to work a double."

"That's fantastic—about the news, not about working a double. What a weird coincidence."

"What coincidence?"

"I just got off the phone with Dr. Crawford. He said he couldn't reach his friend and asked if you'd been able to contact him."

Patrick paused. "It sounds like there's a timeline off somewhere, because we traced a recent cell phone record between Dr. Crawford and Dr. Fulthorpe."

"Wait. They talked?"

"Records show a two-minute conversation."

Something was amiss with this situation. Crawford had had Fulthorpe's number? Then why did Crawford ask me for it? What was he really looking for? Crawford knew something about Fulthorpe. I felt it in my gut.

"I have to go, June. We'll discuss this soon."

"Okay. Good luck. I may be going out this evening to visit a friend."

"Enjoy yourself and be careful. I'll see you later."

Instead of going out to the parking lot, I turned and marched to Aram's office. From the hallway, I saw the light was on, and then it clicked off. Satchel in hand, Aram came out of the room. I stood there like a creeper.

"Oh. Hi," he said.

"Hi."

He waited for me to say something, probably trying to figure out what I was up to. Or had Ursula changed his mind, and he decided to distance himself from me, which would be ideal. We had had our time. We could ever only be friends. But right now, I needed his help and feedback.

"Aram, I was wondering if your invitation still stood, to come to your place tonight? And tackle what is on that flash drive once and for all."

He hesitated.

"I know it's short notice."

"No, no, it's not. I just hadn't expected for you to take me up on my offer."

Was he misinterpreting my intentions? "I don't want you to get the wrong idea. This is strictly work related, right?"

"Yes, that had been my intention as well when I invited you."

My chest lightened. "I feel the info on that drive is significant, and if anyone can figure out what's on it, it's you."

He smiled. "I'm glad you're trusting me in some capacity again. I hope I don't disappoint you."

"Thank you, Aram."

"Would you like to drive with me?" he said. "Or do you still think people who drive BMWs are pretentious?"

I laughed. I'd forgotten I had said that. "Well, it's kinda still true, for those that are."

He chuckled.

"No, seriously," I said. "Thank you for offering a ride, but I have my car."

"I'll order some food. Would you like Thai? Cashew chicken?"

"That sounds good," I said, pretending I hadn't noticed he remembered the special menu item we had shared some time ago.

In my pursuit of answers, I knew I was dancing with fire.

Chapter Thirty-Six

I didn't want to show up empty-handed to Aram's place, so I dropped into a liquor store along the way. The shelves were chock-full of wine choices, and I feverishly scanned row upon row. I found the merlot Aram and I used to enjoy. I picked up a bottle and then thought better of it. I grabbed a cabernet instead.

The GPS led me into a new, upscale neighborhood. I parked on the road in front of a two-story brick house and a nicely landscaped yard. I rubbed my moist palms together. For the sake of justice, I needed to decipher whatever this flash drive contained, and whether it held any significance at all. No matter how I looked at it, I knew my being here could be viewed as inappropriate. But I'd ensure no boundaries were crossed. This was business. Period.

I let out my breath, got out of the car, and climbed the interlocking brick walkway to the front stoop. I rang the doorbell, and in seconds Aram swung the door open. He looked as fit and handsome as ever, with the top button of his white shirt undone.

"Hi," he said and smiled. "Come in." I got a whiff of his freshly applied woodsy cologne.

I stepped inside onto the dark wood flooring. He shut the door, and I handed him my purchase from the liquor store. "For you," I said.

He slipped the bottle from the bag. "Thank you, June. I'm sure it's very flavorful. How about I pour us a glass?"

"Water will be fine for me."

"Water it is. Please have a seat. I'll be right back."

The high ceilings enhanced the spaciousness of the entrance and great room. Twin auburn chesterfields faced each other on an area rug. A glass coffee table sat in between. I eased onto the sofa edge near the fire and admired the marble mantle.

Aram returned with two glasses of water.

"You have a lovely home," I said and took a sip.

"Thank you, June. That's kind of you to say." He sat across from me. "I hope you're hungry. The food should be here soon."

"I am, thank you." I wanted to cringe from the awkward pleasantries of this lovers-to-friends scenario. If he felt the same way, he didn't show it.

The doorbell rang.

Aram clamped his hands together. "Good timing." He stood and answered the door. By his eager reaction, he must have felt a tinge of awkwardness, too. He reached into his pocket for a wad of folded bills and paid the delivery guy, who handed over a plastic bag.

"Keep the change," Aram said and shut the door. "Would you like to eat in the kitchen?"

"Sure."

I followed Aram into the tidy eating area. Overhead, pot lights glowed like soft full moons. He placed the takeout bag onto the spotless black granite island countertop. Aram unpacked the containers of food and removed two plates from the cupboard and cutlery from a drawer. He moved easily, fluidly.

We helped ourselves to scoops of stir-fried veggies, chicken, and rice and sat at the island on bar chairs. In the background, jazz music played. I didn't recall when he had turned it on. I sighed. No, this wining and dining wouldn't work, if that's what this was. I'd been down this path before, and it hadn't ended well.

"Do you like the food?"

"It's really good. Thank you." I crunched on a cashew and kept my eyes on my plate.

"So, fill me in on your ideas about the case," he said.

I wiped my lips with a napkin, relieved to shift our conversation to the topic of work. "I don't have any specific ideas. More of a hunch, really."

He raised his brows and appeared to be intrigued.

His interest in my thoughts bubbled excitement within me, and I continued. "The memory stick, I feel, is somehow pivotal to the case. I think it may give a clue as to why the murder occurred and tell us about David Moreno's involvement. I know you'll have an expert perspective."

He tipped down his chin in modesty and looked at me with those bright aquamarine eyes. "Thank you, June."

"You're welcome, but it's true." I'd always admired Aram's intellect, but I'd have to tone down my appreciation. I didn't want him to think I was leading him on.

After we finished eating, Aram cleared the plates and put them in the dishwasher. He had made an everyday chore look like fun. Maybe it was because he was fun.

"I'll get my laptop," he said. When he came back, he moved his chair closer to mine so we could share the computer screen. He booted up and inserted the USB stick. He appeared to be focused on the case and behaved appropriately, yet I had become very aware of how close we were. Our elbows almost touched.

I started to perspire.

He brought up the files from the drive and then hit the print key. "I'm old school," he said. "I find it's easier to work with a hard copy rather than a computer screen. Just a sec, I'll get the list from my printer."

I wiped my forehead with the back of my hand and quickly fanned my face.

He returned, flipping through several pages. "There are seven and half pages, and about thirty lines per sheet. I'm guesstimating 225 names," he said.

Aram handed me the papers and then logged into St. Eugene Hospital's computer system.

"Okay," he said. "What's the first number on the list?"

I recited the first set of digits, and he typed them in. A patient's profile came up.

"The name matches the one on the flash drive! You were right, Aram. Those are patient ID numbers."

He scrolled. "Here's the name, address, other identifiers, and case history. And it continues. There's a lengthy list of bloodwork, prescribed medications, and treatments. This profile contains comprehensive information."

"Let's try the second one," I said.

He punched in the next case number. The names coincided with the flash drive and the hospital computer system.

"Another match," Aram said and continued checking the rest of the numbers on the page.

"We have a common denominator. All these patients have hematological disorders, and all have been treated by Dr. Stan Fulthorpe."

"That sounds significant," I said and scanned the names on each sheet. "David Moreno had a hematological disorder, but his name isn't on the list."

"No, it isn't. This must be a select group of patients," Aram said. "We have to figure out why these particular people were chosen."

"And then there are two other glaring questions. Why did David Moreno have this list of people's confidential information on a USB, and what was he planning to do with it?"

"Exactly right," Aram said. He continued searching for names and numbers. "See here?" He pointed to an X.

"Does that mean deceased?"

"Yes, it does. You're a smart cookie," Aram said.

I smiled at the cute compliment, then immediately refocused. "Out of curiosity, how many people out of the 225 have died?"

Aram counted the Xs from each sheet. It took a while, but I watched and waited. "In total, there are 152."

"Could that be significant?"

"Possibly," Aram said.

I shelved the statistic in my brain in case we found a lead in this direction later.

"June, I'm going to download each patient file from the hospital system onto one of my own USB sticks, so you have a copy, too."

"Thank you, Aram."

"I'm trusting you with my livelihood." His cheeks dimpled when he smiled.

He made light of what he said, but this was serious. If discovered, a breach of confidentiality could ruin his career and reputation.

"I would never tell anyone."

"I know you wouldn't." We made eye contact. My heart palpitated. He looked away and pushed his chair back. "Do you know what I would like right now?"

I shook my head, a little stunned at the intensity of that brief moment.

"I would like a glass of the wine you brought. Would you care to join me?"

I thought about it.

"Half a glass?" he asked.

I couldn't resist. "Sure. Thank you." He uncorked the bottle. Like a sommelier, his movements were graceful and mastered. He poured some wine into a stemless glass and handed it to me.

I swirled the liquid and took a sip. The rich oak-vanilla flavor stimulated my palate and warmed me from within. My body loosened, and I watched Aram put the rim of his glass to his mouth.

"Mmm. You chose a very nice vintage, June."

"I'm pleased you like it." I took another drink. This sip went down smoother, relaxing me another notch.

Back to business.

"Here's a random thought," I said. "Could the list on the drive by any chance be a compilation of prominent people? Maybe this is a blackmailing scheme."

Aram flipped through the pages of names. "That's an interesting theory. But there's no way of assessing the prominence of these people."

"That's true. What are we missing?" I said, more to myself, and studied the first name on the computer screen, again. Demographics—name, address, phone number, next-of-kin, family physician, health card number. I clicked on the comment box. It read: Primary and sole care transferred from Dr. Fulthorpe to Dr. Crawford, and the referral date.

"Is this normal?" I asked Aram. "To switch primary care doctors?"

"Sure, people switch all the time. They may want a second opinion and end up preferring the other doctor."

"Or maybe the patients think Crawford is a better doctor, or for some reason they don't like Dr. Fulthorpe," I said.

"Possible," Aram said. "But if it came down to bedside manner, Fulthorpe would win hands down."

Patient after patient, I clicked on the comment sections on the list. I finished the first page. "Aram, these *all* say switched to Crawford for primary and sole care."

Aram put his glass down and took a closer look at the screen. He moved closer to me, too.

"That sounds significant, doesn't it?" I said.

He rubbed his chin in thought. "Absolutely it does, but now we have to figure out how it's significant. We still can't rule out a confidentiality breech. Or blackmail, like you had mentioned."

"The question is, for what gain would confidentiality be breached? Or who is blackmailing whom? These may be theories we need to investigate further." My mind spun.

Aram remained cordial. True to his word, he wasn't overtly flirting or making a move. But he looked at me in an intimate way and coaxed forth intimate memories. On the outside I resisted, but inside my body and mind were softening, betraying me. The comfort and familiarity I once had with him surfaced. I couldn't run from it anymore or pretend everything I had felt for him stopped the day he left. My feelings for him never ended. I had buried them deep inside so I could move on.

There. I finally admitted it.

"June? Are you all right?"

It was best to make my exit.

"Yes, I'm fine. How about we take time to think more about all of this?" I shut the laptop and removed the stick. "It's after eight. I better get going," I said. "Thank you so much for dinner."

"It was lovely having you. I will go through these sheets again and see if I can disclose anything."

I grabbed my purse and went to the front door. "Thanks again, Aram. See you at work on Monday."

"Good night, June."

I walked to the car and waved as I drove away. My muscles relaxed. It had taken almost two years to recover from the most aching love loss I'd ever known, and I was grateful how Aram and I had become friends without maintaining any breakup bitterness. But I'd moved on and become entwined in a greater love. My fulfilled heart brimmed with optimism and absolute contentment about my future with Patrick.

But then why did a feeling of unrest, or a sense of incompletion, tug inside of me?

Chapter Thirty-Seven

On my drive out of Aram's neighborhood, my cell phone rang. I saw the number and smiled.

"Hey, Patrick."

"June, where are you?"

I gulped. Come what may, I would keep no secrets. "On my way home. I was just at Dr. Hamid's house discussing the case." I dared not breathe.

"Oh, really? You'll have to fill me in later. Look, my house alarm went off, and I'd prefer it if you stayed clear. Could you turn around and go back to the doctor's place? You'll be safe there."

"But it's getting late. Can't I just go to my duplex?"

"That would be a negative. Want me to call Dr. Hamid and put in the request?"

"No, no," I said quickly. "I'll turn around and ask him. I'm sure he'll understand. He's been very helpful."

"I'm relieved to hear that. I'll keep you updated."

I pulled a U-turn, parked in front of Aram's house again, and turned off the engine. On second thought, I would just wait in the car until Patrick called.

Aram's light was still on, so I assumed he hadn't gone upstairs for the night yet. For about fifteen minutes, I waited and tried to ignore the fact I needed to pee—all that water and wine. I'd go to a donut shop and wait there for Patrick's update. I started the car and noticed Aram's front door opening. He stepped outside.

With nowhere to hide, I turned off the motor and got out of the car. In the shadows, I hoped Aram didn't see me cringe as I walked to up to him.

"Hi. Me again," I said.

He looked confused. "Come on in," he said. "Did you forget something?" He shut the door behind me.

"Patrick's house alarm went off, and he asked me to stay here until it's investigated."

"Patrick's house? You're living with him?"

I nodded. "Yes."

"Come, let's sit," he said and led me to the great room. The couches were more comfortable than they looked. Or maybe it was because I was more tired than I thought.

"And is Patrick agreeable with you being here? With me?" Aram said with concern.

"He's the one who suggested I come back here, if that's okay with you."

"I would hope you know it is more than okay with me." He watched me fidget in my seat. "You haven't told him about us, have you?"

My mouth became desiccated. "Not yet," I said without explaining. "Aram, may I use your bathroom?"

"Of course. It's down the hall. First door on the right."

"Thank you." Soft wall lighting led the way, creating a relaxed and inviting ambiance. I flipped on the bathroom light. Floor-to-ceiling, herringbone marble adorned the room, and an inviting soaker tub sat under a wall-mounted fireplace—a perfect sanctuary to unwind and escape. Like Aram, this house enchanted.

I rejoined Aram in the living room and sat across

from him. He had put two glasses on the coffee table.

"I thought you would like some water."

"Thank you." I took a few sips and sank into the sofa.

"Can I get you anything else?"

I put my glass on the table. "No, thank you."

"How about you lie down and close your eyes?" He retrieved a throw blanket from a chair and put it beside me. "I'll be in the other room."

"You are always so kind," I said and yawned. I closed my eyes and thought I heard him say, "Not always." I placed the fleece blanket on the armrest and tipped onto my side. My cheek rested on a cloud of softness. His gesture had been sweet.

My phone buzzed and startled me. I grabbed it. "Hello?"

"Hey, how are you doing?" Patrick said.

"Good. What's going on?"

"As we speak, there is a crew of detectives scouring my house and the property for any sign of invasion. They're also setting up an electronic perimeter."

"Have they found anything?"

"No, not yet," he said. "I don't know how long they're going to be. Would you like me to make arrangements for you to stay at a hotel, even though I prefer you stay with someone?"

"I can go to one of the motels nearby," I said. "What about you?"

"I'll be on scene here. Please let me know where you decide to stay. And be aware of your surroundings, just in case. Can't wait to see you, this has been a long day."

"Me too. I'll be in touch," I said and hung up.

"You're going to a motel?" Aram had entered the

room without me noticing.

"The crew is still working at Patrick's house. I'll just book something for the night and be on my way."

"Nonsense. I have an extra room."

"Aram, it's not right."

"Okay, you stay here, and I will go to a motel," he said.

I giggled. He continued to bring humor to heavy situations.

"I'm serious, June."

"I can't let you do that." I reconsidered his offer. "Thank you, Aram. I'll camp out on the sofa, if that's okay?"

"It absolutely is."

My catnap had left me wide awake, and I began pondering incessant details of the case. I'd have no complete peace of mind until I had answers.

"Aram, could I please borrow your laptop?"

"Of course." He retrieved it from the kitchen.

"Would you like to sit?" I said and patted the cushion next to me.

He didn't hesitate.

I turned on the computer. The same list of names appeared that I had seen so many times before.

Think, think, think.

"Aram, how about we dig deeper?"

"Deeper how?"

"Into the cases. As a doctor, could you look at the illness of each patient, and the course of treatment?"

"I could give it a try," Aram said, punching in a series of keys.

I started reading. "The first person is a fifty-three-year-old woman. Her initial appointment with Dr.

Crawford was four years ago. She presented with a low white blood cell count and was prescribed a course of medication from clinical trials."

"Now that's strange right off the top," Aram said.

"What is?"

"It's been a while since I was in medical school, but I would have tried Vitamin C therapy. It's the tried-and-true initial treatment for low white counts. And it's vastly less expensive and less risky than jumping straight to an unverified drug."

"Could this be malpractice?"

Aram scrunched his brow in thought. "It may not be the usual treatment protocol, but I wouldn't call it malpractice."

I read on. "The next person is a twenty-two-year-old male, presenting with low-normal platelets and bruising. A bone marrow transplant was performed. Over the next few months, he was treated with platelet transfusions, and told to decrease drinking, and advised against taking aspirin."

"What the hell?" Aram leaned closer to the screen.

His face was only inches from mine, and I inhaled his scent. My heart beat harder, and I suddenly acquired the attention span of a housefly. "Ah, Aram, what am I missing?"

"Sorry, June, I was just looking at the treatment dates to make sure they were in chronological order."

"Do they sound out of order?"

"Yes, completely. From a treatment perspective, Crawford put the cart before the horse. The patient was a heavy drinker and took large quantities of aspirin. His thrombocytopenia was probably caused by his alcohol and aspirin consumption. The first course of action should have been advising against ingesting those substances. A bone marrow transplant should have been a later option." Aram ran a hand over his hair. "That was a risk-filled treatment that may not have been necessary."

"Not to mention expensive," I said.

He sat back. "You are very right."

He read about the next patient. "Seventy-year-old male. Differentials with blast cells. Received the same immune therapy attempts twelve times. Holy crow. Again, these were clinical trials," Aram said.

"Twelve rounds sound like a lot," I said.

"If I was Crawford, I would have switched to another course of therapy after, say, three rounds, especially since there was no notable improvement after any of the treatments. Unfortunately, this patient passed away."

"From these cases, it sounds like you would have handled these patients differently."

"Hematological disorders aren't my area of expertise. Technology has certainly changed since I was in medical school, but yes, I would have used the safest and least invasive methods that have the highest success rates. For example, if someone had a headache, I'd prescribe acetaminophen, not a lobotomy."

"That sounds drastic," I said.

"Okay, I exaggerated a bit, but not by much, actually. Crawford certainly utilizes the newest pharmacological concoctions."

"Wouldn't you?"

"Yes, but only when all else fails."

"That poor man went through twelve rounds of treatment—his hopes dashed after every round. I can't even imagine what he went through."

"I think you just did," Aram said softly. "You're kind, June. Empathetic. And beautiful."

My cheeks grew warm.

"I'm sorry. I don't want to make you feel uncomfortable."

I tensed up and became angry at his apparent kindness, caring, and affection. "Aram, what are you doing? Are you toying with me?"

"No, I would never toy with you."

"Then what are you doing?"

"June, I don't know how serious you are with the officer, but I can't go another day without telling you how I feel."

I froze.

"When we were together, I should have followed my heart instead of my head. After you were gone, my life wasn't the same. I missed you, and I still do."

He had missed me? His soft voice sounded sincere and tugged at my insides. I believed him. I'd always believed and trusted him. "I missed you, too. For so long I had hoped you'd come back."

"It appears fate has brought us together once again," he said.

I nodded. Indeed, fate always had a way of intervening in the most unpredictable ways. Here Aram was, in my life again.

Aram. He had captivated my mind and could always make me laugh. At one time, he had been the center of my world, and could be again.

Black eyebrows and lashes anchored his vibrant, hopeful eyes. His attention intoxicated me. I had craved his love for so long, and now having him profess he still wanted me overwhelmed my senses. My legs became weak.

"What are you thinking?" He smoothed a strand of hair from my cheek. "It's like nothing has changed, isn't it?"

"Yes," I whispered. "I could fall in love with you again. But, Aram, you're wrong. Something had changed. You left me, and that changed everything."

His head dropped.

I realized this was the final closure I needed. I realized now, after spending time with Aram, any possibility of a future together had been severed. I had to unearth my buried feelings in order to let them go. I'd always care for Aram, but my heart and future had become someone else's.

"There is no one else like June Harber," he said.

"And there is no one else like Aram Hamid," I said softly and meant it.

"Thank you." His eyes glistened. "Please excuse me for a moment."

I shifted on the sofa, at peace with my decision. I looked at my phone for the first time. It was after ten p.m. Patrick had texted and had called, too. But my phone hadn't rung, or I hadn't noticed it vibrating. I listened to the message.

"Hey, June. They completed the search of the house. You're free to come over. Call me."

I hung up, and Aram returned.

"Thank you for your help with the case, and your hospitality," I said. "But I have to leave now."

"Are you sure?"

I nodded.

He escorted me to the door and then followed me

outside. We strolled down the walkway, under the stars.

"I relished having you here."

"It was nice," I said. "Thank you, again."

I continued to my car when he gently took my hand. "June—"

Swiftly, his lips claimed mine. They were soft, full, and warm. Familiar, but foreign. I had longed to feel this kiss again. My heart beat fast from the passionate assault, and my knees threatened to buckle. I raised my hands to his chest.

"Aram," I said in a hushed tone, not really knowing what to say next. My thoughts were in a jumble.

Aram's gaze shifted to something behind me, and I turned.

Patrick stood on the sidewalk. Perfectly still. His face was dark in the shadows.

He had seen everything.

Chapter Thirty-Eight

I rummaged in the console between the car seats for a tissue and swerved from the center yellow line. In a flash I relived the one and only time I had crossed into oncoming traffic. It had been after Aram broke up with me. I thought he had wanted to meet me at my car for a secret kiss, but it had turned out to be a sucker punch. He simply watched me become a mess of sobs, snot, and tears.

Was it now over with Patrick and I, too?

I banged the steering wheel with my palms. "No!" This was a different situation. A ridiculous, inappropriate misunderstanding. Would Patrick accept my explanation? Or would I suffer another heartbreak, once again, ironically, precipitated by Aram? Why couldn't Aram have stayed away? I had to be honest. Why didn't I stay away? I hated myself for my behavior. I had toyed with temptation and, until now, thought I had control.

With my sleeve, I wiped my eyes. After Aram's kiss, Patrick's darkened expression haunted my mind. His cold, silent reaction was more unnerving than the revving of his truck engine as he sped away.

When I got to the house, Patrick's truck was already on his driveway, and I parked behind it. I pushed open the front door and crept into the kitchen. He sat drinking a can of beer. My gun rested in the center of the table. My chest tightened, and I wrung my hands.

"Patrick—" I started to explain.

Without looking at me, he cut me off. "You know, I rushed over to Hamid's place to fill you in on significant updates of your case. I tried calling, but I guess you were busy."

"What you saw isn't what you think you saw."

"Here's your gun," he said. "The slug you fired was retrieved from the concrete wall. You're officially in the clear and not responsible for inflicting any injury to David Moreno."

I had prayed for this news. "Thank you for telling me, Patrick. But, please, don't be angry. Let me explain."

He continued talking as if he hadn't heard me.

"The most unexpected confession occurred today, at Lockwood High School. Unfortunately, I can't take credit for this solve. It's funny how there are times when guilty parties implicate themselves." His jaw clenched, and he looked at me, devoid of expression. "In the cafeteria, a sixteen-year-old boy bragged to his friends about his clever techniques of getting revenge on someone who 'screwed his mom' at work."

My mouth slackened. "What?"

"This young man boasted about how he had disabled an engine with a bottle of cola. But his luck ran out when a girl behind him heard his story and told the principal. With impending expulsion, he confessed to the cola crime, and for threatening harm via a note and a broken mirror. It's still to be determined if the mother was in on it."

"Victoria." I shuddered. Her hatred of me ran deeper than I realized.

"The young man will be getting a restraining order to stay away from you and your apartment."

"I would have never guessed this." It hadn't been David, like I'd assumed.

"As for another part of your case, I have a location on Dr. Fulthorpe. He used a credit card out of state."

"That's fantastic," I said and tried to make eye contact. "Patrick, please, talk to me."

He finished his beer. "What's to say, June? Except, Aram's the guy that fucked you up, isn't he?"

"Fucked me up?" I tensed at the crudity. He had never spoken to me this way before.

"I should have suspected when I saw he texted you a couple of weeks ago."

"You looked at my phone?"

"No, June, I wasn't snooping. Your phone was on the bed and buzzed on as I walked by. Funny how timing works, too."

"So, you don't want to talk about what happened this evening? Know my side of the story?"

"There's only one side. The truth. And I saw it clearly."

My heart dropped. I could understand him being angry, but he wouldn't even engage in a conversation. For a man of the law, he was being closed minded for not even trying to hear me out.

"Very well. If there's nothing else, I'll get my things." I went up to the bedroom and took my duffel bag from the closet. I shoved my clothes into it and forced the zipper shut.

Patrick stood at the bottom of the stairs, large, imposing, but he didn't try to stop me from passing by.

"June, don't go," he said in a low tone.

"You don't want me to go?"

"You may still be in danger," he said.

"Well, let's discuss that, shall we?" I tried to keep my voice from shaking. "You just told me the juvenile delinquent that damaged my car and threatened to cut up my face has been busted. And David Moreno, the guy who had broken into my house, is dead. So, I'd say I'm in the clear. Besides." I grabbed the pistol from the kitchen table and held it up by the barrel. "I've got this now. Goodbye, Patrick."

I bolted outside and shoved the weapon into my purse. With so many distracted thoughts, it felt like I was driving blindly. I eased off the accelerator and focused on the road and the color of the streetlights. My phone beeped, but I ignored it until I arrived at my duplex. Only then did I have a look.

—June, please call me if you get a chance. I'm here if you need me.—

The message was from Aram, not Patrick.

I texted back.

—I'm fine. Good night, Aram.—

When I entered my apartment, the box that had contained the cracked mirror sat on the hallway floor. I grabbed it and threw it out onto the front lawn. I locked the door behind me and turned on the exterior light. I checked around to see if everything looked in place, and then I made sure the back door was secured as well.

I didn't want to think or feel anymore. How could I numb the stabbing in my chest?

I rummaged through the bathroom cupboards for a sleep aid and then fell into bed. Sweet nothingness engulfed me until the early beaming sun heated my face. I reached for my phone, and my heart raced a million miles a minute. The message box was empty. No text from Patrick.

I got up and headed to the kitchen. I foraged through the scant items in my refrigerator and found nothing to snack on but wilted celery, spongy apples, and a desiccated piece of cheddar. I tossed them all into the trash. I snatched an open box of wheat crackers and sat on my couch. I munched on stale biscuits in disbelief at how things had ended with Patrick. We had been so close, almost inseparable for weeks. How could he let our relationship vanish, like a puff of smoke? Didn't he want to fight for us?

The one thing I had learned from the last two years was not to dwell on sadness. I'd try to distract myself, at least for the day. My thoughts would be best served trying to bring closure to the David Moreno mystery.

I suddenly gained clarity of what I wanted to do about this case. I dialed St. Eugene's Hospital.

"Hello. My name is June Harber. I would like to speak with Dr. Crawford, if that's possible."

"Are you a patient?"

"No. But I actually may have some information for him. Something he requested."

"Just a moment," she said.

I waited for a couple of minutes and thought my call had been cut off. The phone clicked.

"Gideon Crawford here."

I was expecting to leave a message and was surprised he took the call himself. "Hello, Dr. Crawford. This is June Harber."

"What can I do for you, Ms. Harber?"

"I wanted to let you know, after our last conversation about David Moreno, I may have stumbled upon something."

"I'm listening."

"I found a flash drive in my basement, and I believe David Moreno had put it there. As ridiculous as it sounds, I think he was hiding it for some reason."

"That sounds like an interesting theory. Though I suppose we'll never know since he's gone now."

I regretted my rash decision to call Dr. Crawford. "It sounds implausible, I know. But you're right. I'm sorry to have disturbed you, Dr. Crawford."

"Don't give it another thought, June. By the way, out of curiosity, did you take a look to see what is on that drive?"

"Yes, I did. I believe it contains a list of patient names. They may be your patients, actually. I wondered if you could shed light as to why they would have been listed."

"You got me curious. I can squeeze some time in to have a look. Will you be coming with the officer?"

"No, just myself," I choked out.

"Well, I'm working a half day today. Are you able to come to the clinic at about one o'clock?"

"Sure. I can be there then." I hung up and paced in my living room. What the hell was I doing without Patrick? Was I even thinking clearly? Yes, everything would be fine. I'd ask a few questions and be on my way. Hopefully, he would divulge some information about his partner, Dr. Fulthorpe. I sat on my sofa and scribbled questions to ask.

I checked my phone again. No messages.

Lickety-split, Patrick shifted into reverse and backed out of my life. Apparently without even looking back. And then I thought about it from his point of view.

Would I have been forgiving if I had seen him with another woman?

Probably not.

With no one around, I didn't need to hold back my tears. I deserved this. Not because I let Aram kiss me, but because I let myself believe someone could love me as much as I loved them. I knew this could happen when I let my guard down. Nothing was for certain. Nothing.

I put on black tailored slacks and a long-sleeve crew-neck sweater. I dabbed concealer under my red eyes and brightened my complexion with some blush and lipstick. I looked in my purse to make sure the memory stick was inside. It was beside the gun. I hesitated in checking my phone yet again for messages. I looked at it and then dropped it back into my bag.

No calls. No messages. I was on my own.

After this meeting with Crawford, I was officially resigning from this case.

Chapter Thirty-Nine

I arrived at St. Eugene's Hematology Clinic and parked beside a black luxury Audi—the only other car in the lot. The building's automatic sliding door opened, and I entered. No one occupied the waiting room or the receptionist's chair. There wasn't a soul anywhere, and lights were off in the adjoining rooms. The creepy quietude was deafening, and I didn't know if I should sit down and wait or leave. But then Dr. Crawford emerged from a corridor. I took my phone from my purse, pushed a few buttons, and held it in my hand.

"Hello, Ms. Harber."

"Please, call me June. It looks like everyone is gone for the day."

"Actually, no one else was here. I came in to finish some paperwork."

"Oh, I see. I'm sure it's easier without distractions."

"Please, come this way."

"Oh, sure." I reckoned he didn't like idle chit-chat. I followed him down a hallway and then into a spacious office adorned with an extravagant wooden desk, bookshelves, and leather chairs. Was that an original watercolor painting?

"Have a seat." He closed the door and sat behind his desk. "How about we get started?"

It was obvious he didn't care for me looking around,

either. I scurried into a chair across from him.

"Yes, of course."

"So, you have a USB you would like me to look at?"

"I do, but if you don't mind, I'd like to backtrack a bit about our case."

"I have a few minutes."

In a brief span of time, I knew I didn't care for this man. There was something about him. Arrogance maybe? I'd set my opinions aside. After all, it was cordial of him to meet with me.

"Thank you, Dr. Crawford. Do you remember a few weeks ago when Officer Verbeek and I came to the clinic to speak with Dr. Fulthorpe? That day you told us he wasn't in yet and we couldn't speak with him."

"Yes. It's about the time he went missing. I haven't seen him since."

"Oh, so you don't know he's out of state?"

He broke eye contact with me. "No. I wasn't aware of that."

I probably shouldn't have revealed that information.

"June, how about I get us a couple of waters? Excuse me for a minute."

I must have piqued his interest. He had time to listen after all. He left the office for several minutes. I put my phone face down on the desk and retrieved the memory stick from my purse. When he returned, he handed me an ice-cold bottle of water.

"Thank you very much." I cracked open the lid, took a sip, and put the bottle onto a coaster on the desk. He drank from his bottle.

I held up the memory stick.

His eyes widened. "That's it."

"Yes. I wouldn't have thought of bringing this here,

but when David Moreno was in the hospital, I heard you ask a nurse for his personal possessions. You had mentioned a ball bead keychain. This is on a ball bead chain. Did you know about it?"

He shifted in his seat. "I hadn't said that. You must have heard wrong, June."

I thought for a second. Had I heard something different? I had been nervous that day, while sleuthing in David Moreno's hospital room.

"Dr. Crawford, I've been consulting with the police about this case, and like I said to you on the phone, I think David Moreno hid this in my basement for some reason. I learned he was a patient of Dr. Fulthorpe, and I believe this is some kind of evidence."

"Evidence for what?"

"That's what I'm here to find out."

"May I have a look?"

I handed him the stick.

He inserted it into his laptop and angled the computer so I could see the screen as well. The list appeared.

"These are indeed patients of Dr. Fulthorpe and myself. I recognize them."

I didn't tell Dr. Crawford I knew that already. I didn't want to get Aram in any kind of trouble for having breached confidentiality barriers.

"Some of these people unfortunately have passed away," he said.

Aram and I had figured that out, too. "Do you know why David Moreno would have had this? Did you treat him?"

"No, he was a patient of Dr. Fulthorpe. I don't know how he could have gotten these names. Unless he was

233

some sort of hacker. Or maybe he was trying to blackmail Dr. Fulthorpe for treatment. I know he was a troubled young man, with financial problems."

"Really?" It struck me how Dr. Crawford seemed to know a lot about Moreno.

"Stan Fulthorpe left without disclosing his whereabouts, which unfortunately sounds like suspicious behavior to me. I shouldn't say this, but I know his treatment methods have been questionable."

"How? Has he harmed people?"

Dr. Crawford shrugged. "I'd rather not comment."

That insinuated a resounding yes.

"I understand you don't want to disclose anything. But Dr. Fulthorpe should be reported and held liable if he hurt anyone." Dr. Crawford had presented new angles of the case, angles I couldn't have discovered on my own—such as Dr. Fulthorpe's suspicious behavior, and David Moreno's financial problems.

"I'm only stating possibilities," Dr. Crawford said. "And as much as this pains me, I will look into this situation, and consult with the College of Physicians."

"I'm sorry. I'm not understanding something here. I thought you were treating the patients, not Dr. Fulthorpe."

"Really? Why would you say that?"

"The comment sections say so."

"You've dug deeper into the case files?"

"I had a peek." I underplayed how I had scrutinized the files. "It did appear the patients were given treatments that weren't medically necessary, while many others were put in clinical trials instead of traditional courses of care. And the notations did say you were the primary physician." I suddenly felt a wave of dizziness.

I reached for my water and took a swig. I wiped the condensation from the bottle onto my pants. The wave subsided.

"It sounds like you took an in-depth look at the patients on the USB," Dr. Crawford said.

"To be honest, I did. But I'm glad I came to you to fill in the blanks. We just have to figure out why the comments state you are the primary doctor, if you weren't. It's all the more reason we need to find Dr. Fulthorpe."

He tilted his head as he looked at me, and a shiver ran down my back.

I picked up my phone from his desk. "I should be on my way." My heart quickened when I saw a text. It was from Aram.

—I hope everything is okay with you and the officer. David Moreno's toxicology report came back. His death is suspicious. Call me.—

"Are you feeling all right, June?" Dr. Crawford asked. "Would you like to have some more water?"

"I'm fine," I said, trying to let Aram's message sink into my foggy brain.

"I appreciate you bringing me this USB, June. I will look at all the patient files and review the fraudulent treatments and billings."

"Fraudulent treatments and billings?" I repeated.

Dr. Crawford's emotionless expression iced over.

Alarm sirens rang in my head, and my heart rate skyrocketed. Dr. Crawford had used the words "fraudulent" and "billings," but I never mentioned those words. They were news to me.

Hair on the back of my neck stood on end.

Suddenly I saw Dr. Crawford, the wolf. He'd just

been sheared of his sheep's clothing.
I had to get out of there immediately.

Chapter Forty

"Thank you for your time, Dr. Crawford, but I've kept you long enough." I stood, and a swell of vertigo knocked me sideways. I grabbed the desk for support.

"Are you feeling all right?"

Hadn't he just asked me that? "It's only a head rush," I said as relentless, dizzying waves ensued. I stumbled to the door, but the knob wouldn't turn.

"Why don't you sit back down?"

I realized I'd been on the wrong track completely. It was Dr. Crawford who was guilty of the fraudulent treatments and billings, not Dr. Fulthorpe. And Dr. Crawford had the means and may have murdered David Moreno.

I kept trying to turn the doorknob. Everything blurred.

"June, you're perspiring."

"Unlock the door." I fought panic with labored breaths.

"I can't do that," Crawford said matter-of-factly.

"Oh, my God. You drugged me. Like David Moreno."

"Yes, but he did me the favor of dying."

The room spun. Or was it my head? About to stumble over, I leaned against the wall and tried to dial 911, but the phone dropped out of my hand.

Crawford lunged forward and grabbed it. "I'll get that for you," he said and looked at the screen. "You bitch! You've been recording?" He threw the phone against the wall with a smash.

My mind raced, and I was terrified of losing consciousness. Or dying. Nausea squeezed my stomach, and I took shallow breaths. I reached into my handbag and pulled out my gun. I pointed it at Crawford's blurry form. At close range, I hoped I could hit him with at least one round.

"June, put the gun down. You're delirious. I'm only trying to help." He backed away and picked up the phone on his desk. "It's Gideon Crawford. I need security immediately."

"Open the door!" Blackness crept into my vision's periphery. No. I wasn't going to pass out. I took deep breaths and cocked the gun. I pointed. "Now!" I yelled as loudly as I could.

"Calm down," he said as he approached.

I backed away, out of his reach, as he unlocked the door with a swipe of his badge. My legs shook, and I tried to run out, but gravity pulled me down. I felt a hand trying to pry the gun from my hand.

"Let it go," I heard Crawford say.

I tightened my grip and yanked the weapon away. I aimed at his shadowy form, pulled the trigger, and heard a hollow snap. I fired again. Snap.

The gun hadn't been loaded. Of course, it hadn't. Patrick wouldn't have left it out on the kitchen table loaded.

I was done for.

"You won't be able to prove a thing," Crawford said close to my ear.

With all my strength, I swung my hand holding the gun through the air and smacked something hard.

"Goddammit," Crawford spat.

I tried to crawl away. My last bit of strength drained, and I collapsed onto the spinning floor. I had a vague awareness of activity around me and then felt someone grab my wrists and bind them behind my back. Like David Moreno, I was helpless against this monster, and I'd meet the same fate. I recalled David's mumblings. He must have been trying to warn me, at my house and in the hospital. Why did I come here alone? Even as I entered the building, I hadn't suspected a lone car in the parking lot was a red flag. A lone car. A lone luxury car. I had videotaped such a car the night of the fire. Arsonists like to see their handiwork. Oh, God. Crawford had been at the fire.

A wad of cloth covered my face and pressed onto my nose and mouth. I coughed as I gasped for air. I turned my head and grabbed a breath before my hair was grabbed and the suffocating wad pressed down on my face even harder. I strained my neck but couldn't move from an iron grasp.

This was it.

"Let go of her!" I heard a deep voice say. Patrick. Was it Patrick?

I heard a loud thump, and suddenly my face was free. I could breathe.

"June, open your eyes. Look at me."

It hurt to open my eyes. All I saw was a blur, and then I vomited.

"I need a doctor here, stat," Patrick bellowed. "We're getting you help, June."

Inaudibly, I said, "Thank you."

I had no strength and closed my eyes. Although I couldn't move or see, I could hear.

"Dr. Gideon Crawford, you are under arrest."

Chapter Forty-One

A warm hand held mine, and I opened my heavy eyelids. The world refocused. I was lying in a hospital bed with Patrick sitting beside me, my hand in his. There was an IV in my arm. I felt so tired.

"P—" I tried to say his name.

"Shh," he said. "Rest, my love."

****

The sound of chatter and activity from outside the room woke me. I stared at the plain beige ceiling and struggled to remember everything that had happened in Dr. Crawford's office.

A nurse came into my room. "Good morning, June," she said in a soft tone. "Do you mind if I turn the light on?"

"No, not at all."

She pulled the cord to turn on the wall light and then peeled the tape from the back of my hand. She removed the IV needle and pressed a gauze pad over the small puncture. "How are you feeling, dear?" she said.

"I feel well," I said, surprised by how well I actually felt.

"No dizziness or nausea?"

"None," I said and looked at the empty chair beside me.

"He never left you all night."

"Who?"

"The officer." The nurse taped up my hand. "Your bloodwork is normal. After the doctor signs your release papers, you'll be free to go."

"Do you know what happened to me?"

"Apparently, you were drugged. We gave you fluids to help flush them out. There's no rush, but when you're ready to get dressed, you'll find your belongings in the locker."

"Thank you," I said. When she left, I swung my legs over the bed and adjusted my hospital gown. In socked feet, I made my way to the locker and washroom. I supposed I'd call a taxi to take me home to my duplex. The sooner the better.

Had Patrick really been here?

After dressing, I stepped out of the washroom, and there he was, standing beside my bed. A thousand hummingbirds fluttered in my chest. My legs became shaky, and I put my hand on the back of a chair. He rushed to my side.

"I'm fine." I made my way to the bed and sat on the edge. I was afraid to ask the next question. I didn't enjoy seeing him frown. "Why are you here?"

Patrick cleared his throat. "Since the night you left my house, I haven't stopped being concerned about your safety. How are you feeling?"

I shrugged. "Still alive."

He ran a hand through his hair. "Damn it, June. I was worried sick. Why the hell didn't you call me?"

Heat rose in my face. "Why would I have called you? To tell you the door hit me on the way out?"

"May I sit?" he said.

"If you want."

He pulled a chair closer. "The other night, I never wanted you to leave."

"Funny, your actions showed otherwise."

There was a knock on the door. A slim, middle-aged man in a coffee-colored suit walked in. He looked at me with sympathetic brown eyes.

Patrick took my hand. "Are you up for a visitor?"

"I think so."

"Hello," the man said in a soothing voice.

"Hi." I wondered who he could be.

"Hello, Officer." The man shook hands with Patrick. "June, I'm Stan Fulthorpe."

"Dr. Fulthorpe," I said, stunned. The elusive Dr. Fulthorpe. "It's a pleasure to meet you. I, we, have so many questions."

"I'll do my best to answer them. I owe you that."

"Please have a seat, Doctor," Patrick said.

The doctor sat in Patrick's vacated chair while Patrick stood.

"First," Dr. Fulthorpe said. "I want to apologize for how you've become involved in these tragic circumstances. This whole situation went awry quickly."

"How did this all happen?" I asked.

"It happened because I shouldn't have trusted someone, a colleague, a friend. Or so I thought." The man appeared distraught. "I'm sorry. I don't mean to be vague. Long story short, my ex-partner jeopardized the health of patients and defrauded insurance companies."

Few things angered me more than a person of power taking advantage of the vulnerable. "I'd like to hear the entire story, if that's okay."

Dr. Fulthorpe nodded. "As you know, Gideon Crawford and I run the hospital's hematology clinic. We see our own regular patients and often cover for each other. About five years ago, I followed up with one of Gideon's patients. After reading the case history, I was startled to see how Gideon had treated this patient."

I shifted. "In what way?"

"I'd describe the treatment as unethical and risky."

"You mean like inappropriate use of clinical trials?"

Dr. Fulthorpe raised his eyebrows. "Along with performing excessive, expensive procedures, that's absolutely what I mean."

It was exactly what Aram had surmised.

"Dr. Crawford didn't follow treatment protocols. When I approached him about the matter, he agreed with my sentiments, but continued using unconventional methods. I decided then and there I wouldn't co-treat patients with him. That's when I started documenting cases."

"And transferred the information onto the USB drive?" Patrick said.

"Yes, onto three USBs, actually. And onto the cloud," Dr. Fulthorpe said. "I hid the USBs in the ceiling tiles of my office, my home, and rental house."

"That's why David hid the drive in the ceiling tile at my place," I said. "But why did he choose my place?"

"He was being pursued and needed a safe place to hide the USB, and himself. Your place foot the bill."

The pieces were falling into place. It seemed nothing happened by accident, but by design or some reason.

"I had confronted Gideon about his malpractice. This time, he didn't admit any inappropriate care. He even attacked my methods. I told him if he didn't report himself to the College of Physicians and Surgeons, I would. As long-time colleagues, and the godfather to my daughter, I made the mistake of giving him a few days to get things in order. That night my house and office were ransacked, and two of the three memory sticks were stolen, and somehow the information on the cloud was erased. Gideon had certainly hired hard-core mercenaries. I'm sure they're the ones who burned down my rental home to ensure no evidence remained. And then hunted down poor David."

My mouth had become dry, and I tried to swallow.

"Would you like to rest, June?" Dr. Fulthorpe asked.

"No, please go on," I said and took a sip of water. "Who was David Moreno?"

The doctor continued. "He's a young man I'd been caring for, for over a decade."

I glanced at Patrick and frowned.

"David struggled to pay for his medications, and more times than not, I hadn't charged him. He had insisted on repaying me somehow, so on a whim I asked him to retrieve the last and only remaining USB drive from my rental home. I scribbled my address on a card for him. And then when he went there, well, you know what happened next. Evidently, he and I were being watched. When the thugs tried to steal the USB from him, it ended in a deadly struggle. David bled profusely because of his illness, and that's when you and the officer came on the scene. He knocked you down and snatched the bloody towel, reclaiming his own DNA evidence. Trying to protect me from being implicated."

"Poor guy," I said.

"I never would have asked him if I'd have known of Gideon's malevolence. That's when I knew my life and my family's life were in jeopardy and I had to stop Gideon from hurting his patients. My wife, daughter, and

I escaped to Florida, and from there, I reported Gideon and arranged for his arrest while clearing my name. Thanks to the help of Officer Verbeek."

"I respect what you did, Dr. Fulthorpe." Patrick put a hand on my shoulder. "It's not easy being a whistleblower."

Patrick's gesture warmed me inside. I knew he referred to what I had done, too.

"I appreciate that, Officer. And thank you for all your help. June, I'm sorry you got caught up in all of this. I should have handled it better."

"I believe you handled as best as you could," I said.

"I should be on my way and let you rest," Dr. Fulthorpe said.

"Thank you for telling us everything," I said.

"Thank you, Doctor," Patrick said. "I'll walk you out."

I took another sip of water. In a few minutes, Patrick returned and sat next to me.

"The man is carrying a lot of weight on his shoulders," Patrick said.

"He has a conscience."

Patrick nodded. "Yes, he does."

"Well, this really is all over now." I glanced at my bag on the ground. "I guess I'll be on my way home."

"June, wait."

I remained still, unable to guess what he was about to say. His expression hadn't betrayed him in any way.

"June, I want to beg for your forgiveness."

Air rushed from my parted lips. "My forgiveness?"

"I don't know what happened between you and Doc Hamid, and I don't care. I mean, I care, but not enough to lose you."

I wanted to cry with joy. Even when Patrick didn't know what had happened between Aram and I, his feelings for me hadn't wavered.

"You just have to tell me, June, which one of us do you want? I mean, I wouldn't blame you if you choose Hamid. He is obviously a great guy. Highly scholastic. Not bad looking."

This was the first time I heard Patrick ramble. I put a finger to his lips to stop him from talking. "You were right about what you said. Aram was the one who had 'effed me up.' "

Patrick lowered his head. "I shouldn't have said that."

"But you were right. Aram and I used to be involved. I thought we were happy until he broke it off. I hadn't seen it coming. It happens, right?"

Patrick nodded. "It happens."

"That's when I decided it wouldn't happen to me ever again and I focused on work, not dating."

He thought for a bit and then shook his head. "And all those times I had asked you out, I thought you didn't like me."

"It wasn't personal."

"Why did you finally agree to go out with me?"

I shrugged. "Because I missed my bus."

"Yes, I recall that well. I have to thank that bus driver for running ahead of schedule that day."

I thought for a moment about an enormous revelation. "Patrick, until that day, I'd been holding out on life, on love, on you. I have to thank that bus driver, too."

Chapter Forty-Two

The next morning, I awoke nestled beside Patrick. Just the two of us—nothing between us—no secrets, ties, or handcuffs. Not anymore. Not ever again, unless…

"Patrick, I still have so many questions. What's happening with your job? Are you in danger from that previous case?"

"The force is tracking the situation. We'll continue being cautious, vigilant, the opposite of what you were when you went to see Crawford. June, what possessed you to go there alone?"

"I went alone because we were broken up."

He sighed.

"I want to explain what happened these past couple of days, starting with the evening I was at Aram's."

"Tell me, my love."

"When I had told you I'd be at a friend's house for the evening, that friend was Aram, which you already know."

I peeked at Patrick to see his reaction, but he remained immobile with a poker face.

"Aram and I were on the computer all evening, looking at the files on the flash drive. Case by case, reviewing results. He behaved appropriately, but then we reminisced. I made it clear how you and I were together. When I left, he followed me outside and kissed me. It was then I knew."

"Knew what?" Patrick stroked my arm.

"He wasn't you."

I sensed honesty, love, and passion glowing in Patrick's deep blue eyes. He was all I wanted, and I snuggled closer.

"After that horrible night, I went back to my apartment, distraught about having lost you. Thoughts about the case circulated in my head, and I recalled something distinct when I went to the hospital to visit David Moreno. Dr. Crawford had been in David's room and asked the nurse for David's personal possessions, and if he had a ball bead keychain. That detail struck me as being very specific because the USB had been on a chain just like that.

"The next day I called Dr. Crawford and told him I had a memory stick and asked if he'd look at it and give his opinion about what it contained. He suggested we meet at the hospital, which sounded logical. Never would I have imagined he was evil. But then when I got to the clinic, nobody was there. I got a weird sensation inside.

"We chatted; he gave me bottled water. I cracked open the lid and drank a few sips. As I was about to leave, he said he'd look into billing discrepancies and fraudulent treatments. But I hadn't mentioned anything about either. Suddenly, I knew something was very wrong, and I had to get out of there. But I became very dizzy. Things are hazy after that."

"Because he drugged your water." Patrick's body tensed.

"That's one thing I don't understand. When I opened the water bottle, the seal cracked open. How could the water have been drugged if the cap hadn't been tampered with?"

"The bottled water was analyzed. It contained a high concentration of GHB—gamma-hydroxybutyrate—the date rape drug. And the bottle had a pinprick hole in it. Crawford had used a needle and syringe to inject the drug into the bottle to keep the cap intact so you wouldn't suspect anything."

"How could I have been so naïve? Sorry I botched things up."

"No. You did quite the opposite. While drugged, you managed to tape a murderer's confession and save yourself from being potentially murdered. You single-handedly caught a ruthless criminal."

"What if you hadn't shown up when you did?"

"It doesn't matter. I'm impressed by how you decked Crawford with a gun to the jaw," Patrick said. "I can see the headline now. Lab scientist turns badass crime fighter."

I shook my head. "Hardly. You're the hero. In every way."

"I was just doing my job. In dealing with people, I've seen the worst in many and how easily people will lie, steal, and hurt others, without conscience. And then I met you with your nose in your work. Focused, with an amazing work ethic. I asked you out, and you said no. I knew you were the one for me. I just had to convince you."

"And you did," I said and kissed him on the nose.

"You've been brave through all of this, and even in prior times when you had the courage to report your underhanded co-worker."

I shook my head. "You make it sound like I was decisive and fearless, when all along I was uncertain and terrified."

"You rose to every difficult situation, and I won't let you downplay what you did when times were tough, and what you went through. You, June Harber, are heroic. I want to love you until the end of my days, if you'll have me."

My eyes moistened. "Patrick." I kissed him with all the love and tenderness in my heart. "I want to spend my life with you, too."

He wrapped his arms around me, and he kissed my lips, cheek, hair, neck. I laughed, elated.

A question popped into my mind. "Patrick, how did you know I was with Crawford?"

The flurry of kisses stopped. "Ah." He scratched his neck. "I installed a tracking device under the driver's seat of your car. I also monitored your phone's GPS."

"What? That sounds so creepy." But I wasn't angry. He was a cop, protecting me, and, as proven, the situation had warranted it. "So that's how you knew I was at St. Eugene's Hospital."

Patrick nodded. "Tracking you was the only way I could have let you leave. Gad, I'm a stalker."

I giggled and then became curious about something. "Patrick, you know my dating backstory, and I'm wondering about yours. All that time you were trying to go out with me, did you date many women?"

He shook his head. "No."

"No, not many?"

"None at all."

"How was that possible? I mean, you're so hot."

Patrick chuckled and sloughed off the compliment. I didn't think it was possible, but his modesty made him a hundred times more attractive. And sexier.

Amusement left his face, and he stared off.

"What is it?"

"About the time we met, I was bogged down with work, and dealing with a back injury."

"I'm so sorry. I had no idea."

"You couldn't have known, babe. Thankfully, it's much better now," he said. "It's the reason I wasn't very 'pleasant' the day we first met."

I caressed his chest as he spoke. "I remember that day. I thought you were a jerk. I'm sorry I judged you wrongly."

He kissed the top of my head. "Don't be. I was a jerk. But the truth is, after meeting you, I became disinterested in pursuing anyone else. It's why I suggested you take a job with police forensics. What could have been a better way to get to know you?"

I snuggled closer. I remembered the countless times I had rejected him. "I never made it easy on you. Thank you for not giving up on me. You are my one and only love. Never doubt that. But—"

He froze. "But what?"

"On your next case, could you count me out? I'd prefer to work in a safe, predictable, controlled lab setting."

"Whatever you want. Anything. Anyhow."

I raised a brow. "Do you mean that?"

"I do," he said firmly.

"Good." I reached under the pillow and pulled out a pair of handcuffs. He smiled, knowing the "drill." He didn't hesitate to extend his arms. I bit my bottom lip in anticipation. I held up my hand and locked one end of the cuffs onto my wrist.

"There's been a change of plans, Officer. Are you

willing to engage?"

Passion brewed in his eyes. "Affirmative. Ready and able to engage, my love. Now and forever."

A word about the author...

Prior to writing, Judy was a professional figure skater and toured with the International Holiday on Ice Revue. After graduating from college, she became a medical laboratory technologist and worked in clinical chemistry and anatomical pathology. Her current focus is to create stories with interesting plots and characters she hopes readers will enjoy.

Judy loves spending time with her family in Ontario, Canada.

www.judymalcolm.com

Thank you for purchasing
this publication of The Wild Rose Press, Inc.

For questions or more information
contact us at
info@thewildrosepress.com.

The Wild Rose Press, Inc.
www.thewildrosepress.com